James Warden was a teacher for forty years, and retired in 2006. He now enjoys his retirement as much as he enjoyed his time in the education service, and is catching up on those things which he left undone and ought to have done – in particular, his writing. He writes every morning between nine o'clock and noon, for thirty-six weeks of the year.

He is fortunate enough to be able to act in several Norwich theatres – the Maddermarket, the Sewell Barn and, with the Great Hall Players, at the Assembly House – and this experience informs his writing. His stage adaptation of Laurie Lee's *As I Walked Out One Midsummer Morning* was performed at the Sewell Barn Theatre in November 2009. His original play, *Letters from a Boy in the Trenches*, which was based on the letters of a WW1 soldier, was performed in Marchington, Staffordshire in 2015.

James is married – for the second time – and lives in Norfolk. He and his wife travel as much as possible. They have visited Italy (where they were married in 2002) several times, Canada, Bermuda, Egypt, India, the Czech Republic, New England, Poland, Slovenia, Antarctica, the Falkland Islands, Alaska, the Galapagos Islands, and Australia. They have also taken several holidays in various Mediterranean resorts – the basis for his first novel, *Three Women of a Certain Age*, which was published in July 2010.

During his years in education, he wrote about twenty play scripts for children. These included the one that formed the basis for his children's story, *The Great Gobbler and his Home Baking Factory at the North Pole*, which he wrote in 1982 and published in December 2010.

He has three sons by his first marriage and they inspired two of his novels – *The Vampire's Homecoming*, which was published in 2011, and *The One-eyed Dwarf*, published in 2012. With them and his first wife, he also travelled to the southern states of North America, France, Germany (West and East), Estonia and what was Czechoslovakia.

Other Writing by James Warden

<u>Stories of Our Time</u>
Three Women of a Certain Age (2010)
The Age of Wisdom (2015)
Swinging in the Sixties (2016)

<u>'Tales of Mystery and Imagination'</u>
The Vampire's Homecoming (2011)

<u>Stories for Children</u>
The Great Gobbler and his Home Baking Factory at the
North Pole (2010)
The One-eyed Dwarf (2012)

<u>Biography</u>
The Boy in the Photograph: Bill Pieri's autobiography (2014)

<u>Plays</u>
As I Walked Out One Midsummer Morning (2009)
(Adapted with the permission of Laurie Lee's estate)
Letters from a Boy in the Trenches (2015)

THE FIRST
RENDLESHAM
INCIDENT

by

JAMES WARDEN

**Grosvenor House
Publishing Limited**

All rights reserved
Copyright © James Warden, 2017

The right of James Wardento be identified as the author of this
work has been asserted in accordance with Section 78
of the Copyright, Designs and Patents Act 1988

The book cover picture is copyright to James Warden

This book is published by
Grosvenor House Publishing Ltd
Link House
140 The Broadway, Tolworth, Surrey, KT6 7HT
www.grosvenorhousepublishing.co.uk

This book is sold subject to the conditions that it shall not, by way of
trade or otherwise, be lent, resold, hired out or otherwise circulated
without the author's or publisher's prior consent in any form of binding or
cover other than that in which it is published and
without a similar condition including this condition being imposed
on the subsequent purchaser.

A CIP record for this book
is available from the British Library

ISBN 978-1-78623-083-6

To my old friend, Dave,

remembering his 'little library in the sky'

Chapters

Principal Characters

Dave Roach

Sir Robert Hargreaves
Lady Geraldine Hargreaves
Myles Hargreaves: their son
Patricia Hargreaves: their daughter

Agnes Ward
William Ward, farm labourer, Agnes's husband
Tom Ward: their son
Rachel Ward: their daughter

Harry Cole: farm labourer and poacher
Jack Stevens: local policeman
John Bird: local farmer
Amanda Bird: his wife
Norman Bird: his son
Steve Lomax: forester

Emma Barber: housewife
George Barber: Emma's husband, teacher in Woodbridge school, Roach's cousin

The gent from Chillesford

Lieutenant Colonel Pat Humphreys: Deputy Commander of USAF Bentwaters
RAF Chief Controller (Neatishead)
PC Heath

Sally Tigg: a writer

Glyn Owen
Glyn's girlfriend: a nurse
Gwynfor Evans

The CPO
The statesman

Louis
Kaamil: friend of Roach's

The year is 1955

Preface

This story is based largely on the diaries kept by my friend, Dave Roach, during his time in Butley and the years that followed. We came to know each other during our National Service, and then went our separate ways: I, following a degree course, to civil engineering for Staffordshire County Council and Dave to ... well, let Roach tell his own story – or, at least, the major part of it.

As I say, we had gone our separate ways, keeping in touch only through Christmas cards and the occasional visit to each other's homes, although these became more infrequent as the years passed and Dave withdrew further and further into himself and the nightmare he had uncovered. It was a surprise therefore to receive a letter from his solicitors, Cadge and Gilbert of Radlett, saying that I had been named in Dave's will as his executor.

It was while I was going through his papers in the March of 1980 that I came across the diary. I opened it with some reluctance at first: after all, a man's diary must be considered a private matter between him and his god. But the story, scrappy though it was, held me. I shall always remember looking up from the final page and finding myself alone in his Borehamwood flat with a full moon as the sole illuminator of his account.

I settled his affairs but kept the diary to myself, locking it away in the top drawer of my desk. What it had to tell seemed no more than the ravings of a madman, even after the events later that year, which are now widely known as the Rendlesham Forest Incident.

It wasn't until I retired in 1995 that I opened his diary again. My wife had died that year after a bitter battle with duodenal cancer (an event that precipitated my retirement) and I needed taking out of myself. Distraught beyond mere grief, I travelled to Butley where I found an excellent bed and breakfast establishment run by Mrs Langdon. Sensing my state of mind, she was more than kind to me and I spent that spring immersed in the village and its people. All remembered Dave and the events of the summer of 1955 and many were prepared, forty years on, to share those experiences.

Even so, I was reluctant to commit pen to paper and a further five years were to pass before I did. At the turn of the century, I opened my laptop and told my old friend's story (with more regard for its narrative order than he was able to do in his diary) over the autumn of that year and the winter of the following. I then closed it again. Told in the third person to include things I had discovered that Dave could not have known at the time the story seemed more fantastical than ever – fantastical and dangerous.

Now, as I turn 80, I feel that if I do not publish, nobody will. I have changed the names of those who do not wish to be identified and left vague the location of some places of importance, but I have been scrupulous in adhering to the facts of his account. Believe Roach's story if you will or ignore it if you will, but his story should, at least, be told.

CHAPTER 1

The disappearance of the children

It was the final week of the summer term and classroom activities were winding down at Butley Primary School: lessons were more or less abandoned for the pleasures of the playing field. On that particular morning the children who hurried along the country roads from the surrounding villages were looking forward to their sports day.

Sir Robert Hargreaves's children, Patricia and Myles, usually met up with the Wards at the fork in the road known as Wantsiden Corner. Patricia and Myles were privately educated, of course, but spent their summer at the family home, which stood across the heath and only a short walk from the village. Since their school finished early, Patricia and Myles were allowed to attend the local primary school for the last two weeks of the term. Tom and Rachel Ward liked the Hargreaves and spent much of their own summer up at the "big house" (as their mother called Sir Robert's country home) and, sitting on the verge at the side of the road, had waited anxiously for Patricia and Myles.

The weather had been hot for several days and by 8.30 that fateful morning the sky was already free of clouds and stretched a clear, bright blue from the distant woods to the cornfield that bordered the road – a fact that later threw considerable doubt on the children's account of what happened. To be completely accurate, it must be said that only Rachel witnessed the actual disappearance of Patricia because Tom was carving away at a piece of twig, while she gazed

3

along the track that led across Wantisden Heath; but it was Tom who ran towards Patricia when his sister cried out and it was Tom who felt the force of what he later described as "the extraction", comparing it to the sensation one feels when a tooth is pulled.

The Hargreaves had been running hell for leather down the track, calling out to their friends, when Patricia's voice was culled from the air. One moment she was yelling excitedly on seeing Rachel, but the next was nowhere to be seen. Myles looked distractedly around and then he, too, simply vanished. Tom by this time had almost reached his friends only to be lifted to a height of about ten feet in the air before being dumped back on the ground. "It was like having a bad tooth pulled," he said later, "You know – the empty feeling when there's nothing there, just the hole."

By the time Rachel reached her brother, other children were converging on the spot from the main village street and Church Road. Some of these children later confirmed Tom's story, saying they had seen him drop back to the ground; and one girl supported Rachel's account of seeing both Patricia and Myles "hovering in the air like dragonflies".

The shouts of the children brought their teacher running from the school house with her hands still wet from washing the breakfast dishes. Rubbing them dry on her apron as she ran, the teacher gathered the children together and soothed them gently into silence.

"One at a time," she said in honoured fashion, "and then I shall be able to hear you."

When their stories were completed and excitement had been replaced by fear, she led them into the schoolroom and sat everyone down, while other children arrived from neighbouring villages. She was unsure what to do. The stories were obviously nonsense but the children seemed so convinced of their truth and it could not be denied that Sir Robert's children were missing – quite an unusual occurrence since they always enjoyed their short sojourn at the village school.

Finally, she decided that the best course of action was to send Bert Higgis, the local blacksmith, to the Hall where he could report the matter to Sir Robert in person.

By the time they both returned on horseback, the teacher had extracted several variants of the central misadventure from the children – and was more confused than ever. Sir Robert listened with what she construed as ever-growing alarm and then advised her to inform the local constabulary so that a search might be organised. He would, he said, return home and arrange a search of the grounds where, he felt, his children were certain to be found.

"I'm sorry to have put you to all this trouble, Miss ... but I'm sure that they have just run off – playing truant, hmm?" he laughed.

"They were looking forward to sports day, Sir Robert ..."

"I'm sure, I'm sure ... but don't concern yourself, Miss ... er ... don't concern yourself. I'm sure we'll find them, and then I'll give them a piece of my mind for the worry they've caused."

With that assurance, he re-mounted his horse and galloped away across the fields, and Bert Higgis returned to his forge and the horse he had been shoeing.

The morning rolled on with still no sign of the two children: no word was heard from Sir Robert and the local bobby reported that a thorough search of the roads and lanes leading back to the Hall had proved fruitless.

When Tom and Rachel went home at lunchtime and told their mother, Agnes Ward, of the incident her only comment was to the effect that they should "eat their dinner and not fill their heads with nonsense". Nevertheless, after they had gone back for their sports day, Agnes took a stroll along the heathland track and looked carefully at the ground for several hundred yards from where it joined the Woodbridge to Orford road. What she was looking for wasn't apparent at the time even to her, but she remembered, vaguely, something Harry Cole, the poacher, had said and it was this that provoked her examination of the spot where the children had been said to disappear. Satisfied with what she found – or didn't find – Agnes turned back towards the school where sports day waited and her children were expected to do well.

That night, at The Oyster Inn, William Ward, Tom and Rachel's father, listened to the gossip of the men and, in particular, to the comments of Harry Cole, who either knew more or less than he was saying. William was inclined to think less: in his experience, Harry Cole liked the sound of his own voice. He might be a good poacher – and you could be sure of a decent night out with him – but that was about the extent of his reliability. Back home, William did little more than grunt when his wife enquired whether or not he "learned anything", and then went up to bed, leaving her to tidy round the house. William was a farm labourer; it had been a hard day and tomorrow would be even more so with the harvest approaching faster than usual after so much warm weather.

"You're not worried about the children, then?" Agnes enquired once she was in their bedroom and placing her hairnet carefully over the curlers.

"No," was all he'd say, and she knew him well enough to realise there was no point in pushing him for further information.

Up at the Hall, Sir Robert no doubt gazed out across his domain and wondered. He had bought the place and restored it, reclaiming centuries of an English tradition that had given the world the landscaped garden. He had always hoped to restore some of its more community minded traditions: fox hunting, harvest suppers, May Day ceremonies and summer fetes. Now, his children were missing. Deep down – very deep down – his natural anguish was, somehow, assuaged. But there was no one in whom he could confide – not even his wife: especially not his wife who the local doctor had dosed and sent safely to bed.

Jack Stevens, the local bobby, spent much of that night cycling along the roads and tracks that led in and out of the forest. They were not comfortable walks – not even on a summer's day. He'd always put it down to the conifers: there was something stark about conifers, which offered none of the sense of well-being he associated with deciduous trees – the blessed oaks, elms, ashes, birches and beeches he loved so well. Having crossed the heath, Jack made his way to Friday Street, turned south past the Old Rookery and so through the Hundred Acre and Tangham Walks. There was no sign of the children; there was no sign of anything. He dropped off at the farm where he knew a hot cup of red tea would be waiting if he was dry: John Bird didn't sleep too well and always welcomed a visit.

"Nothing out of the ordinary," he replied in answer to Jack's question, "Just the usual sounds and noises. Those planes get on my nerves, coming and going. I wish they'd just go."

"No more funny happenings, John?"

"None," was the abrupt reply.

A strange thing had occurred a few months before. John's eldest boy had appeared at the top of the stairs, having asked to go to bed early one evening, and had seemed to stumble forward. At the critical moment – just when the boy seemed sure to strike his head in the fall – he slowed down and floated into his father's arms. "I couldn't have reached him before he hurt himself. I just prayed," John told his wife afterwards as they sat at breakfast, "He did a complete somersault and landed in my arms."

"He hasn't talked about playing with his friend in the woods anymore?"

"No."

Jack wished the farmer good night, listened for a moment to the cosy snufflings of the cattle and cycled on through Capel St Andrew and so to Butley Abbey, where he rested again – rested and sat to think. His own children had talked about meeting "a boy or girl" (they didn't seem sure of the sex of the stranger) and floating up and over the roads and fields.

"We held hands, Daddy, and just floated up in the air," they'd said. Childish talk, naturally: there's nothing like the imagination of a child. But now, the Hargreaves children had actually vanished. According to their school friends, they'd been sucked up into the air. "Extracted like a bad tooth," was the expression Tom Ward had used.

At breakfast the next morning, William Ward turned to his children and frowned severely, the knife that had just sliced through a thick rasher of bacon poised in his hand.

"You go straight to school today – no hanging around, and when school finishes you come straight home. You understand me? And don't you go up to the big house. You hear me? If I find you've disobeyed me, I'll take the strap to you, Tom. You understand? You look after your sister."

"Yes, Dad," Tom replied, knowing full well that whenever his father mentioned the strap he was deadly serious. His father had never strapped him (although the same couldn't be said of other fathers in the village) but Tom knew that when it was mentioned his father was making a point as firmly as possible. William's knife punctuated the air as he turned to Agnes.

"You're off to town today, aren't you?"

"It's market day."

"I know. It can't be helped."

"I thought you said last night ..."

"I know what I said last night, but you can smell it in the air. It's like a storm brewing. When I was out feeding the pigs this morning, I saw Jack Stevens. He'd been out all night and found no sign of them children."

He turned again to Tom and Rachel, his knife carving patterns in the air.

"You mind what I say. You come straight home."

"Emma Barber's taking the children home for lunch," said Agnes, eager for there not to be a row.

"Hmm ... good. There'll be safe with her."

On Nathan Catchpole's coach to Woodbridge (the coach was always referred to as "Nathan's" because it was always the same coach he drove, although he was simply the driver), Agnes Ward suddenly remembered why she had been impelled to take a look at the track where the Hargreave children had vanished so mysteriously.

It definitely had been something Harry Cole told her one day. According to Harry, he'd been collecting firewood from the forest when he came on some strange marks on the ground. They were dents as though some heavy object had stood there for a while. "The odd thing about them," he'd said "was their shape. It were a triangle". He was wondering what could have caused them when he became conscious of being watched. Looking behind him into the trees he saw nothing at first, but then became aware of eyes on stalks and limbs that reminded him of the stems of plants. There was a kind of fluttering and the crackle of wings and then two children ran off laughing. He'd shouted after them, but didn't know who they were or he'd have had a word with their parents. It wasn't much of a tale and Harry Cole couldn't be trusted anyway, but it did make Agnes feel uncomfortable.

CHAPTER 2

Roach comes to Butley

Dave Roach arrived in Butley on Nathan Catchpole's coach when it returned the womenfolk from Woodbridge market. He had travelled up from London on the train to Ipswich and then caught a connection to Woodbridge. Roach had been invited to spend some time with a cousin and his wife. His cousin, George Barber, was a teacher who cycled the dozen or so miles into Woodbridge to work each day. He and his wife, Emma, had found a derelict cottage down by Butley Creek and had told Roach in a letter that they were 'doing it up'. Roach had offered to help.

Roach had served his two years National Service in the RAF, and it was while we were together in Sharjah on the Persian Gulf that we became friends. We took to each other immediately, although more or less anyone would have become friends in Sharjah, which was known as "the arsehole of the world" at that time; camaraderie was high on everyone's list. The insects known as "shit beetles" were everywhere and everything one did one did on the camp; there was simply nowhere to go. A ten minute jeep ride to Sharjah took you to a scattering of broken-down, ramshackle huts on the beach, and the people were poorer than church mice. Roach's trade was that of wireless operator, while I was responsible for the de-salinisation unit, which processed all our drinking water from the sea. There was nothing to do off-duty except drink and chat in the NAAFI, and neither Roach nor I drank much in those days. To occupy our time, we both took an interest in photography at which Roach became very skilful and was eventually given the job of camp photographer.

He was a very amiable chap and was soon in conversation with the women on the bus. One of these was Agnes Ward, who walked him down to Butley Creek when Catchpole's coach arrived in the village. Tom and Rachel were sitting at Emma's makeshift kitchen table eating their tea, which consisted of Welsh rabbit and a glass of orange juice. Welsh rabbit was a speciality of Emma's; she somehow managed to blend milk and tomatoes with the cheese to produce a dish that was both smooth and succulent. When she created the same meal for me, while we talked forty years later, the taste caused me to think of Roach as he entered her kitchen, saw the children eating away and noticed the look of relief on their mother's face.

"Don't worry, Agnes – they're safe," Emma said with a smile.

Roach had been regaled with the story of the disappearance of the Hargreaves children as Catchpole's coach wended its way along the Suffolk roads, pausing at the numerous villages for the women to alight with their market produce.

"You obviously introduced yourselves," replied Emma, smiling. She and Roach had only met once, and that was at her wedding to George. She felt that Agnes Ward might know her guest better than she did herself.

"Mrs Ward and I have had a long chat on Mr Catchpole's coach," answered Roach, turning to Agnes, "Would you like me to walk you back?"

"No. No thank you, Mr Roach. We'll have to get used to this until those children are returned."

"You think they will be found?" asked Emma.

"I honestly don't know, Mrs Barber, but I hope so … I just can't imagine where they could be."

"There are no mine shafts in this area, are there?" suggested Roach, "There's nowhere they could be trapped?"

"They disappeared into thin air, Mr Roach – thin air. Just you ask my Rachel. I must go now. Bill won't be pleased if he arrives home and his tea isn't on. Mind you, it'll be a late night tonight – they're harvesting. Thanks for looking after them, Mrs Barber."

Agnes hustled her children out through the kitchen door and Roach and Emma were left feeling high and dry in each other's company.

"George will be a while. Would you like a cup of tea?"

"I'd love one. I stopped drinking it in Sharjah. The NAAFI couldn't make a decent cup of tea to save their lives. "

He sat down at the small, wooden table and stretched his legs.

"George told me that you were in the RAF."

"It seemed romantic at the time – and, to be fair, I enjoyed my National Service on the whole. I made some good friends, got away from home for two years, learned a trade and built up my confidence."

"What was your trade?"

"I was a wireless operator and I also got the chance to study photography. Since there was no official photographer on the camp, I was given the job."

"What are you going to do now you're out … Dave?"

"Help you get this place in order," he laughed.

"No – I mean eventually," Emma replied, placing the large brown teapot on the table and filling Roach's cup.

"I think there might be openings in the photographic industry. We'll see. And I could always operate a switchboard or I might get a job with the BBC... This tea's good. I love it strong so you can taste it."

"There are some scones I've made. Would you like one?"

"I'd love one. Home cooking! George is a lucky man."

"It's still hard. He cycles a dozen miles to work each day because it's cheaper living out here than in Woodbridge, and teachers aren't paid a great deal. We're wondering if we can afford a family. But we are a lot better off than the farm labourers like William Ward."

"I noticed Mrs Ward's children were patched and darned all over."

"Most children have their school uniform and very little else. Their playing-out clothes are always old school clothes or hand-me-downs from relatives or friends. I used to wear my older sister's jumpers whether they fitted or not. Mum never threw anything away. And the older the clothes get the more patches they have – especially in the seat of the boys' trousers!"

Roach remembered feeling over-privileged as he sat listening to Emma Barber. There had been no girls to look good for in camp and nothing to spend his money on, and so he'd arrived back in England with a tidy sum in his pocket and had stopped off in London to purchase some decent, smart outfits. Money hadn't seemed too short in the capital. He recalled visiting some friends in Windsor and finding the shops there (and not only the clothes shops) to be well stocked. In one, he'd come across a group of Eton schoolboys – very smartly dressed in their stiff, white collars, top hats and tailcoats – talking to an elderly shopkeeper as though he was a servant. Roach had balled them out in no uncertain, military fashion.

"These scones are good," he said, smiling at Emma and tucking in.

"There are compensations to living in the country. Don't stint in helping yourself to the jam. We make our own and there's always too much."

When he had finished eating, and the ice had broken between them, Roach suggested that they took a look at the old cottages Emma and his cousin had chosen as a home. One kitchen was in decent repair, albeit in need of extensive decoration, but the rest of the properties were in a poor state. One might have been proof against the elements, but it was barely habitable. George and Emma had found them on a cycle ride out from Ipswich. They were three derelict, thatched cottages that Roach assumed must at one time have belonged to fishermen and their families because they were situated on Butley Creek, a salt water tributary of the River Ore.

"We're hoping to knock them into one," said Emma, at first with a smile and then with a laugh, "The locals think we're crazy."

The surrounding 'gardens' were overgrown with nettles and all three of the original front doors were loose or broken down. Most of the windows were smashed but had been roughly boarded up by George

"Children playing," suggested Emma, raising her arms in a helpless gesture.

The cottages had simply been two up, two down, giving George and Emma twelve small rooms in all. The better of the three cottages had a usable room for a bedroom and the kitchen in which Emma had welcomed Roach, and there was another room in the end cottage that Roach could use as his bedroom.

"It's fortunate we've had a warm summer," he said with a smile.

"You don't mind? It is dry!"

"No. I'm looking forward to the challenge, especially if you keep providing me with tea and scones. Seriously though, I can see the place has potential, and you do have one huge advantage ..."

"Which is?"

"You're very close to the electricity wires that must supply the village. We'll get in touch with the Electricity Company and see if we can have those tapped. If we can – and we will, believe me – you'll have electricity once we've installed a transformer. You'll then be able to run everything on electricity, including a pump for this garden well."

"We'll be better off than some of the homes in the village," said Emma, and for the first time since they'd met Roach saw real joy in her eyes.

It was as they were talking by the well that George arrived. He parked his bike against one of the dilapidated walls, stuffed his cycle clips into the pocket of his sports jacket and rushed towards Roach, hand outstretched.

"You like it?" he asked as they shook hands.

"I prefer your wife's scones," replied Roach, responding to firm grip of his cousin.

"You wait until you've tasted tonight's supper. It's Wednesday. It must be ... liver and bacon! Am I right?"

George turned to his wife, and kissed her lightly on the cheek.

"Why don't you show Dave the village while I get supper ready ... and show him where the children were supposed to disappear."

Roach – who had listened with close attention to Agnes Ward's account of the disappearance of the Hargreaves children, which had been supplemented by the opinions of the other women on Mr Catchpole's coach – had had his own curiosity aroused sufficiently for him to want to investigate the site of the happening.

When they arrived at the spot on Wantisden Heath that drew Agnes Ward the previous morning, Roach and George soon found the marks to which she had referred. They were faint by now and overgrown (Harry Cole's story had been set some time ago) but there were marks if you wanted to find them.

"What do you make of Harry Cole's story, George?"

"There are two marks and they are vaguely triangular in shape. If these were the legs of an aircraft, there would have to be a third somewhere. Supposing them to be equally spaced ..."

George rooted around – shoving gorse bushes aside and poking through the bracken that grew prolifically on the heath – while Roach sat and filled his pipe from a chamois leather pouch. After twenty minutes or so George called Roach over and pointed at a third mark.

"What does it mean?" asked Roach.

"At a guess – no, an estimate – I would say that the three marks were the landing pads of a circular object, which – judging from the distance between them and allowing for an overlap – suggests a craft measuring about forty-five feet in diameter."

"You mean one of these flying saucers!"

"On the other hand, the three marks could be completely unrelated, and be nothing more than rabbit scrapes," replied George, laughing.

Roach elbowed his cousin in the ribs and pushed him over into the bracken. They larked about for a while as they had done as boys, pushing each other around and thumping each other in the chest before Roach suggested that they should sit and have a smoke. He relit his pipe, loosened his tie and began to talk.

"I think these children will turn up. I ran away as a child. Didn't you? *But I think we need to keep an open mind about these things.*"

"There've been stories about flying saucers in the papers over the summer – they've nothing else to write about, I suppose – and it's captured people's imaginations," replied George, pulling away quietly on his cigarette.

"I suppose you put Rachel Ward's story down to a child's imagination?"

"I don't know, but I do know the power of women's gossip. Yesterday was a bright, sunny day and the sky was blue. None of the children mentioned a flying saucer, which they couldn't have failed to see in a clear sky. I just think we need to keep our feet on the ground and find a rational explanation."

"Yes," answered Roach, exhaling calmly.

"Don't tell me you think there's more to this disappearance than a childish prank?"

"I said I think they've probably run away, but the women on the coach did say that your village bobby had spent last night searching for them and was out again early this morning – in vain. I would have thought they might have turned up by now."

"Come on Roach. You're not telling me you think that Robert Hargreaves' children have been snatched by little, green men?"

"No, that's not what I'm saying!"

"You don't sound convinced."

"I know nothing about the children's disappearance, George, but there are 'stranger things in heaven and earth', as they say."

"Go on."

"During my time in the RAF I met several pilots, naturally, and stories do circulate – very discreetly – among them about strange, flying objects: aircraft that simply cannot be identified as being in the normal run of things. A Flight Lieutenant I knew – ordinary sort of chap, no imagination to speak of – once told me that he had seen what he believed to be what the papers call a 'flying saucer'."

"You'd been drinking?"

"Not that much. I drank very little when I was in the RAF."

"Go on."

"It was about five years ago – clear summer's day, a bit like today – and he was walking across the airfield towards his quarters when he heard what he described as 'a humming sound'. He turned and saw what looked like a discus – the kind of thing we threw on sports day. It was travelling in a straight line and as it came overhead the humming sound intensified and was accompanied by a distinct crackling noise – the kind of noise you get when high voltage electricity jumps a gap. The disc was light grey in colour and it reflected the sunlight. The edge of this disc was quite distinct, and the main body of the craft seemed to be rotating within it. The edge was certainly a different colour from the main body and was a mass of sparkling lights. Apart from those lights the craft had no other external features: no windows, no doors, and no portholes. My friend said that it must have been flying at about 800 feet and travelling at somewhere between 500 and 900 miles per hour. He estimated that it was probably about 100 feet in diameter."

"I take it that he reported the matter to his senior officer."

"As a matter of course – yes."

"And?"

"He was brought before some committee or other – a sort of working party – who questioned him intensely for several hours at the end of which he was told not to ask questions of them or anyone else about the matter, not to make enquiries at the Air Ministry about who they were or what their official standing might be and not even to discuss the matter among his comrades in private."

"What did your friend think it was?"

"He is a professional pilot. He sticks to the facts. He knows what he saw, but leaves speculation to the newspapers and your gossips."

"But what does he think?"

"He says, quite simply, that in his opinion the craft was not one that could have been designed and built here on Earth."

"And you believe him?"

"What reason would he have to lie?"

"Impressing his mates, making a name for himself, seeking the limelight? It could be any of those."

"Yes, it could. I suppose none of us is averse to being the centre of attention," replied Roach, and added "Let's hope those children are found soon," as though he wanted to change the subject.

Both men sat quietly for another ten minutes or so, and then George stood, stretched his arms, straightened his legs and suggested that they return home for supper.

Darkness was settling in nicely and a kind of peace pervaded the dingy kitchen as the last rays of sunlight filtered in through the lattice window over the sink. They sat talking after Emma's dish of liver and bacon with mashed Maris Piper potatoes and greens smothered in rich, onion gravy had been devoured. The talk was about the renovations to Creek Cottage, as Emma now called their intended home, and neither Roach nor George mentioned Roach's story or the subject of flying saucers.

Instinctively, they both felt that the little woman needed protecting from such worries. Writing now, all these years later, their attitude sounds condescending, but it wasn't a matter of condescension. Emma's role as housewife and prospective mother was central to the home and the future of all, and it was their duty, as men, to shelter her from the fears and tribulations of the outside world. Even now, after the unparalleled social changes of the last sixty years that I have welcomed, I can appreciate their view.

"Why don't you go across to The Oyster for a pint," suggested Emma as she cleared the dishes from the table.

"Emma," said Roach as he struggled to his feet with his stomach bursting, "Is there any chance that you can find me a wife like you among your friends? The liver and bacon was extraordinary – just like my mother used to make – but to top it with plum duff and custard was a master-stroke. Thank you."

"It's a pleasure, Dave – I may call you Dave? I love cooking. I learned the art at my mother's knee. She used to shoo my brothers outside to play, and she and I would settle down in that little kitchen in Pauline Street in Ipswich to cook. We baked once a week and I couldn't wait to get home to help her with the supper. We children always had high tea – Welsh rabbit or eggs on toast – but she cooked supper for Dad and her, which they had when we'd gone to bed. This was after the war, of course. Dad was away during the war."

"On active service?"

"Yes. He was in the navy – the submarine corps – but he never talked about it."

"No, none of them did."

A short walk across some rough pasture that bordered the cottage took George and Roach to Mill Lane and thence, after about a mile, into the village and the welcoming sight of The Oyster pub. As he had said, Roach wasn't a drinker in those days and George rarely visited the pub on his own: it was only if a friend cycled over from Ipswich or Woodbridge that he ventured in for a pint. It wasn't considered quite fit for George to be seen drinking, him being a schoolmaster, and he respected the constraint.

As they pushed open the door of the bar, therefore, the two men were greeted with silence and the stares of a dozen or so not overly-friendly faces. They weren't immediately welcome; acceptance would have to be earned. Roach, whose confidence had been boosted greatly during his years of National Service, smiled broadly, nodded a greeting to all and sundry and elbowed his way between two men who dominated the bar.

"Do you sell mild?" he asked, "Mild was one thing you couldn't get abroad in the forces. IPA by the gallon, but mild – neither hide nor hair."

Whether he intended it as such or not, I cannot be sure, but it was a speech that established his reputation in the village as an outsider to be reckoned with and respected. The very mention of his being "in the forces" and having served "abroad" was enough to establish his credentials.

"We do, sir," answered the landlord, "Would that be two pints?"

"No," said George, picking up on Roach's approach, "I'll just have a pint of the usual."

They found a table and sat down, while Roach surveyed the bar. There were, of course, no women present: the local was an exclusively male abode. It was a dingy place but cosier than the NAAFI. On that warm, summer evening the windows were open but the smoke from the men's cigarettes and pipes still created a deep haze across the room. There were a few scrubbed, deal tables around which the old boys sat playing dominoes. A group of younger men stood to one side of the bar playing darts. Roach commented to George on how that particular sound – the light treble thud of the darts in cork – reminded him of the NAAFI at Sharjah.

The pint of mild was sweet and rather warm and there was the faint taste of the wood from the barrel in which the ale had matured. Roach looked up at the dark, low ceiling and across at the fireplace where, in winter, a log fire would roar. Even now, in the middle of a hot summer, the room was cool and the men wore their trilbies or flat caps. Some had a neckerchief and a few had donned a tie for the evening out. All were smoking hard and clutching their glasses of beer down the inner sides of which the foam slid.

Two men in particular caught Roach's attention. One had arrived soon after Roach and George entered the pub and now sat alone at the end of the bar. He wore a flat cap pulled down firmly on his head and had a long scarf criss-crossed over his chest. This scarf was tucked into the top of his trousers. He wore a waistcoat from whose pockets dangled the chain of a watch fob. His shirt sleeves were rolled partway up his arms so they covered the elbow but did not obstruct the wrist. The belt around his waist was at least four inches wide and did nothing to hold up his trousers because it hung down over a slender abdomen. As the man leaned forward to raise his glass, Roach noticed a pair of braces protruding from beneath the waistcoat. Around his lower legs the man wore a pair of leather gaiters that gathered in his trousers and rested on his working boots. On his right wrist there was a wide, leather band such as archers wear. He looked as though he had just come from work or was about to leave for the same, whereas everyone else was simply out for the evening. Roach marked him down as Harry Cole, the poacher. When he whispered the question to George, his cousin confirmed Roach's impression.

Without hesitation and completely out of order, Roach picked up his pint and walked over to the man.

"Mr Cole, I presume," he said, in mock reference to Stanley's greeting of Livingstone.

"You might presume what you like. And who might you be, may I ask?"

"My name's Dave Roach. I'm George's cousin. I've come to help him refurbish Creek Cottage."

"You've got a right job on there then. I wish you luck."

Roach's direct approach had quite startled the Oyster regulars who liked their introductions to take more time – preferably months or even years – and every ear was now on the conversation between Roach and the poacher.

"I understand, Mr Cole, that you've had one or two odd experiences with regard to strange marks on the ground and strange rustlings in the undergrowth."

"I daresay we've all had those when we were younger," answered Harry, catching the attention of the room.

"But yours were unsettling?" persisted Roach, ignoring the laughter around him.

"Some were, I dare say," replied Harry to more quiet laughter.

"I travelled up on Mr Catchpole's coach. The women told me what you'd seen."

"Did they now?"

"They were quite full of your stories."

"Were they now?"

"Yes, they were," answered Roach looking very directly into Harry Cole's eyes: a gesture that seemed to unsettle the poacher. "Well?"

"You don't want to pay any attention to the gossip of women."

"I've found the gossip of women to be an avenue to certain knowledge."

"Is that right?"

"Will it lead us anywhere?" Roach asked.

"Will what lead us anywhere?"

"The gossip of women," said Roach with a smile.

"They've got nothing better to do on market day."

"But was there anything in what they said?"

"Maybe there was and maybe there wasn't."

"It would be helpful to know."

"I daresay it would."

Roach paused, but stared stubbornly into the poacher's eyes. Eventually, when neither had blinked, he offered to buy Harry a drink. The poacher hesitated for a moment and Roach continued to stare him out, realising that it might be a long evening if the conversation continued in its current vein.

"I don't see why I shouldn't have that drink," said Harry at last.

"Good," replied Roach.

"What's your interest, anyway?" asked Harry when Roach had placed the poacher's usual in front of him.

"I was in the RAF. I have an interest in flying machines."

"Who said anything about flying machines?"

The question was fired quickly at Roach and in a bad-tempered voice. In fact, the response was so sharp in tone that several of the men shifted uncomfortably in their seats. They hadn't come here for an argument, but a peaceful evening away from the wife. The most uncomfortable of all was Harry Cole, who immediately began to sweat and bite his lower lip. Before Roach appreciated what was happening, the man began to shake feverishly and tears sprang from his eyes.

"I ain't saying nothing. What I seen ain't fit for decent conversation. You buy a man a pint – that don't mean ..."

He seemed unable to articulate his feelings, and Roach reached for his arm in what was meant to be a soothing gesture, but Harry pulled it away and struggled from the stool. It was at this moment that the other man Roach had noticed stepped forward to intervene. As with Harry, it had been the man's mode of dress that caught Roach's eye.

It wasn't so much that the man's purple waistcoat seemed odd any more than did the dark, corduroy trousers or the knee-length, leather boots; and it wasn't the hat, which seemed to be a cross between a trilby and a top hat, or the long yellow coat. In their way, these accoutrements were no odder than Harry Cole's getup. It was the velvet collar that seemed completely out of place in a 1950s pub in Britain; it was almost as though the man was of another age. He spoke in an old, soft voice: a voice that soothed and controlled.

"I have some medical knowledge," he said, "Is our friend ill?"

"I'm all right," said Harry, "I'll get home now. I'd better be going."

Without another word, he downed his pint and left the bar. The other man nodded to Roach, smiled around the room and followed Harry into the night.

"Who was that?" asked Roach.

"The gent lives over at Chillesford. He drops in occasionally. Enjoys walking," the landlord offered by way of explanation; and with that, Roach and George had to be content.

CHAPTER 3

Road Block

Roach woke early the next morning with a stiff neck and badly-aching shoulders. Not only was he uncomfortable, but he had hardly slept at all, and the less manly part of him was already beginning to regret the offer he had made to help George and Emma restore their cottage.

Emma's breakfast, however, soon bolstered his determination. He had heard that country people tended to fare better than their urban cousins during the wartime rationing that had lasted until the previous year. When he rose from the little table in Emma's kitchen, Roach believed it to be true. A plentiful supply of eggs helped, of course, and Emma seemed to have chickens running everywhere.

George had left for work earlier, and so Roach got on with the task of clearing the debris that had accumulated around the three cottages: broken bricks, rotten beams, window frames, door jambs and pieces of lead pipework. It was hot work for the sun had risen early, and by mid-morning Roach was ready for the large glass of homemade lemonade that Emma handed him.

"George is going to be so grateful," she said, "He's really too tired at night, after a day's teaching, to tackle this mess, and that only leaves the weekends."

"It's a pleasure. All we had to do in Sharjah was to sit around and chat. I'd forgotten how fulfilling physical work can be. I'll chop this old wood up for winter fires and store it under the lean-to at the back by the coal bunker. We can smash the bricks into rubble to form a base for your paths and those downstairs rooms that will need re-flooring."

Roach worked through until lunch by which time he had cleared the surrounds of Creek Cottage of the nettles, bracken and brambles, and had a fire smouldering away in the rear garden.

"Do you like corned beef? It's all we have, I'm afraid. I can make a sandwich," said Emma.

"Love it. Why people complain about corned beef I don't know. It comes a close second to Spam as far as I'm concerned."

"You're teasing me."

"Not at all! Before I was called up I lived at home and my mother always cooked me Spam fritters on a Friday night."

"What work did you do before your National Service?"

"I didn't. I was lucky enough to get a place in grammar school, and I was there until I was eighteen. I volunteered for National Service. The theory was that volunteers were paid more and had a choice of posting. It was more or less true."

"And you chose Sharjah?"

"Not exactly. My first posting was to RAF Eastleigh …"

"In Hampshire?"

"In Nairobi, East Africa. It was a lovely camp – five thousand feet above sea level on a plateau. It was the perfect climate – just pleasantly cool."

"So how did you end up in Sharjah?"

"I was trained as a wireless operator, but teletape is replacing Morse code – which is what I'd learned to use – as a means of communication. Fewer and fewer camps are using it, and they're the backwater ones like Sharjah. The RAF sent me where I might be of some use."

Emma listened in amazement at this young man who seemed to have done so much, while she had simply fallen in love and married George. She'd trained as a secretary after leaving school but was now a housewife; not that she minded being married, but life as a secretary had put her a cut above the rest of the girls and she'd enjoyed working alongside her friends in the typing pool.

"I take it that all your water is heated on that old kitchen stove?" asked Roach, cutting into her thoughts.

"Yes, even for bath night we heat the water, saucepan by saucepan."

"Are you planning on having a bathroom?"

"There's no running hot water anywhere in the village."

"But there could be. If we get the electricity put on here, you could have a boiler installed."

"And a proper bath instead of the tin one we keep in the coal shed?"

"Yes."

"Luxury!" laughed Emma, suddenly realizing there might be more to housewifery than she'd been thinking, and that she ought not to regret her decision to marry. Forty years later talking to me about their conversation that day, Emma said that Roach's presence over the summer had relieved the loneliness of living in the countryside and rallied the belief she held on her wedding day that she and George had a future in the village. It was, after all, a good place to raise your children.

By late evening, Roach had ripped out the broken-down parts of the fence and re-fixed the rest, the gate swung on its hinges and the one blackberry bush that promised fruit had been pruned back to a manageable shape and size. He and Emma stood in the garden admiring his handiwork and wondering what had become of George.

"He's always late but never as late as this," Emma was saying just as George cycled into view.

"Sorry," he shouted, resting his bike against the newly-restored fence, "Have I spoiled supper?"

"No, but where have you been?" answered Emma as she kissed him on the cheek and took his sports jacket from his shoulder.

"The main road is completely shut off for traffic. I've had to cycle all the way round through Capel. It was the same this morning. I was almost late for work."

"Why is the road shut?"

"I don't know. Jack Stevens was there but it's the Americans who seemed to be in charge. Road blocks both ends cutting off access to the Hundred Acre and Tangham Walks."

"Perhaps we could wander down after supper and take a look," suggested Roach, "I'm rather averse to our roads being closed to Englishmen by the Yanks."

"But first, supper," urged Emma, "Steak and vegetable ragout. It's been simmering all afternoon. Agnes bought me the stewing steak from town yesterday. I know you like it ... Oh and we get to eat the steak. During the war, Mum told me that she always left the steak in one piece, removed it from the stew and used it for other meals later in the week so that what you got was steak-flavoured peas and beans."

"Times have changed," laughed George, "and for the better. But first I'd like a quick wash. I'm covered in dust and sweat from that cycle ride. I won't be a moment."

"There's a pan of hot water waiting on the stove. I'll give you a hand."

Roach stayed in the garden, while Emma helped George with his ablutions. When he had washed his face and neck, and his arms to the elbow, in the bowl of hot water Emma handed him, George stepped outside to call Roach in for supper, re-knotting his tie as he came.

The meal was simple but filling: the small pieces of steak had been well and slowly stewed and the peas and broad beans added bulk and flavour. The dumplings, soft and moist, reminded Roach of his mother's cooking, and he said so, much to Emma's delight.

After supper, Roach and George wandered down to the village. Just beyond the parkland known as The Thicks they came to the roadblock mentioned by George. Jack Stevens was no longer there but an American serviceman stood on sentry duty. Beyond the barrier he guarded, George and Roach saw a number of jeeps and other military vehicles parked by the roadside at the edge of the forest. What the occupants of these vehicles were doing was unclear, but they seemed to be examining the contents of various boxes – some quite small and one that was as long as the munition boxes Roach had become familiar with in Sharjah. They had pieces of apparatus slung from harnesses on their shoulders. None of them looked up as the two men approached, so engrossed were they in their work.

"How long is this road to remain closed?" asked Roach, in that direct and disconcerting manner he adopted when dealing with any kind of official.

"I've no idea, sir."

"My friend has to cycle to work in the morning, and it's rather a long way round. Is it likely to be open by then?"

"I can give you no more information, sir," replied the serviceman.

"You are ...?"

"I'm a security police officer, sir. I work at the base."

"RAF Bentwaters?"

The man frowned for a moment as though he thought Roach might be questioning American ownership of what was, in fact, a British air-force base, albeit on loan to the United States as part of the NATO agreement.

"We're in close touch with your police force, sir."

"No doubt," replied Roach, "but your use of the base does not authorise you to close off the forest, does it – or, indeed, even enter the forest without permission from our authorities?"

"I wouldn't know about the regulations, sir."

"Oh, I think you do, officer. Moreover, you have no right to refuse me entry to the forest, do you?"

George was becoming more and more agitated by Roach's manner and the obvious discomfort of the serviceman whose mood was shifting rapidly from annoyance to anger.

"Excuse me, sir," he said with careful politeness, as he slipped the mouthpiece of a walkie-talkie device from its holder. There was a crackling sound as he flicked the switch that brought the microphone to life and then he said "I need assistance at the barrier."

George noticed a senior officer glance up from the large box, have a word with his colleagues and then stroll towards them.

"I'm Lieutenant Colonel Humphreys. How can I help you?"

"It would be helpful to know when this road is to be opened. I cycle into Woodbridge for work each morning," replied George, before Roach could cause any more offence.

"We hope to have it open by tomorrow morning, sir, but can't make any promises. In the event of the road remaining closed we shall provide military vehicles at both barriers in order to facilitate the movement of the civilian population."

George caught the smile on Roach's face as they listened to the ultra-politeness of the American officer's reply. He was a young man but seemed to be an experienced officer: his calm manner diffused Roach's irritation visibly.

"May I ask what has happened?" asked Roach.

"Indeed you may, sir. One of our aircraft was forced to crash land last night. Fortunately there were no casualties, but there's a considerable amount of debris in the forest that would prove hazardous to anyone entering the area. Once we've cleared it we shall, naturally, reopen the road. If that's all, sir, I need to get back to my duties."

"Yes, thank you," replied Roach, mollified.

Walking back along the road towards Butley, he turned to George.

"If we follow the Capel St Andrew road out of the village we should be able to make our way into the forest shouldn't we?"

"It would be simpler to head north across Wantisden Common, skirt Staverton Park and try to enter the forest that way – assuming, of course, that the road isn't lined with military personnel. I take it you don't believe Lieutenant Colonel Humphreys?"

"I'm just curious as to what happened. Nothing more."

"And you don't think we're likely to be arrested? I have to get to work tomorrow," George asked with an uneasy laugh.

"We'll be careful. When I was at RAF Eastleigh in Africa, we used to go over the perimeter fence at night – I won't go into details, but local girls were involved at one and sixpence a time – and the MPs must have known, but they did nothing about it. Do you understand, George? Sometimes, it's best to ignore what is going on – especially if stirring the water disturbs the mud at the bottom of the pond."

Wondering why Roach wasn't following his own advice, George led his cousin along the little stream west of Butley and so to the area of farmland that bordered the forest. The light was fading by now and the moon was rising in a darkening sky. From where they stood the Butley to Woodbridge road was clearly visible and all seemed quiet. The land, in fact, belonged to John Bird, who Jack Stevens had visited following the disappearance of the Hargreaves children. It was mainly arable land but John kept some dairy cows. These were now grazing peacefully and George wondered whether anything could be amiss in this gentle, pastoral setting. A light was on in the farmhouse and Roach suggested that they should have a word with John Bird: being so close to the forest, he might have seen or heard something the previous night.

"I saw nor heard nothing," he said, pouring them a cup of the red tea favoured by Jack Stevens, "but my cows did. I was damn lucky not to have lost the bloody lot. They were all over the place. Damn near had heart attacks, the lot of them. Running about they were as though demented. You ever seen fear in an animal's eyes? I have. They're only cows, I know, but I ain't in favour of frightening them to death."

Back on the edge of that part of the forest known as the Hundred Acre Walk, Roach turned to George and asked him whether he wanted to go on. George didn't. The story of the cows had unnerved him, and the atmosphere was unsettling. There was a silence about the woodland he could not quite place until he realised that it was the lack of animal noises he noticed. Even at night, there is usually the sound of something: a fox prowling, rooks settling, rabbits feeding.

Here, there was neither sound nor movement. However, he smiled, reassured Roach and together they crossed the road and into the forest.

The darkness of the pines closed about them as they made their way as noiselessly as possible towards the part of the pine forest that was contiguous to The Thicks. They eventually found a path that acted as a firebreak. After a walk of a mile or so, they heard the sound of men's voices. George felt his movements become slower and slower as though he was walking in a dream and struggling to wake. He looked at Roach who seemed unaffected. The voices grew louder and they saw lights and heard the unsteady crackle of what Roach later told George were Geiger counters. Tests for radioactivity were being conducted. The pines were too thick for them to see anything other than shadows moving back and forth in the glow of the arc lights. If they were to get closer and remain invisible to whoever was working under the lights the two men would have to leave the path and risk the snapping of dry twigs beneath their feet, but such sounds might go unnoticed in the restrained mumbles of conversation and unrestrained cracklings beyond the pines. Roach whispered that he felt it was worth the risk and they were looking for as silent a route as possible when the sound of a rifle bolt being drawn back and slid into place brought them to a swift halt.

"Stay exactly where you are or I shall be obliged to shoot," said a quiet voice.

They heard a brief exchange on a two-way radio followed by the sound of running feet and turned slowly to find Lieutenant Colonel Humphreys smiling at them from the forest path.

"I thought you might be curious, gentleman, but I'm afraid that this is as far as we can allow you to go. I can assure you that we do have full permission from the British authorities to be active in this area. Should you have any doubts I suggest you contact Squadron Leader Blakemore in the morning when the village post office opens. I can give you his number if it's of any help."

George smiled to himself, relieved at the American's bantering tone. He guessed there was to be no comeback for what would be seen as trespass.

"Perhaps my men can escort you to the Woodbridge road and we'll be pleased to offer you a lift back to the village."

The Oyster beckoned them as they alighted from the military jeep and Roach and George were soon downing a pint of "the usual" watched with slightly less reservation than on the previous evening by the locals; talk was of the road blockade, and their arrival in an American jeep was a matter of great interest. It was already common knowledge that Roach was a RAF man and it was supposed that he might know more than he was "letting on". No one asked any questions – this would have seemed discourteous – but the air in the pub was tense with curiosity. Eventually the landlord called from behind the bar, where he was polishing glasses:

"You gentlemen get lost?"

Chuckles reverberated around the bar at the impertinence of the question, which was designed to loosen Roach's tongue. He rose from their table – that is, the table on which they seemed expected to sit because that is where the landlord had placed their pints, since they had chosen it on their first night – walked to the bar, turned (leaning back with his elbows on the bar) and addressed the room.

"Gentlemen, we know little more than you, but I'm only too happy to share our experiences this evening."

He did, building a picture for the locals of strange goings-on in Rendlesham Forest and the unwelcome presence of American forces. Memories of the war years were still pervasive at that time. The slogan applied to the "yanks', as they were called, during the war – "overpaid, over-sexed and over here" – was still current. After all, local girls had taken up with them and many had left to become wives and mothers in America. Besides, once the war was over and the men had returned the Americans tended to drink on the Bentwaters base, preferring chilled beer to the warmer British version.

They were only seen in The Oyster nowadays if they were involved with a local family, and that involvement wasn't always welcomed.

When Roach finished speaking the bar was silent as each man digested what had been said; there was barely a murmur as George ordered their second pint. Dominoes clicked on the wooden table tops, and darts thudded once more into the board; but the games were now secondary to the thoughts of the men. Women would no doubt have opened up the conversation and speculation would have been rife, but the men of Butley supped their pints and mused.

As the silence thickened with the pipe and cigarette smoke, George noticed that Harry Cole was not in his usual place at the end of the bar, and he asked his whereabouts.

"Harry don't always come in but I was expectin' him tonight," replied the landlord, without explaining why he expected Harry on that night in particular.

After a while, having downed their second pint, Roach and George rose to leave, bidding goodnight to the regulars and receiving a reassuring murmur in response. As they paused at the road junction – Roach to light his pipe and George to breathe in some fresh air – another man emerged from the Oyster and called out to them.

"Mr Roach, I'm Bill Ward" he called, "You met my wife yesterday."

"Mr Ward, pleased to meet you," replied Roach, offering his hand, "Yes, your wife was telling me about the disappearance of the Hargreaves children, and then she took me down to my friends' house at Butley Creek."

William Ward nodded a greeting to George and then took both men aside.

"I heard you ask about Harry. He's in a bad way, Mr Roach, a bad way. If someone of your knowledge could have a word with him it might help."

"How do you mean – 'a bad way'" asked Roach.

"I'd rather he said. He was due here tonight but wouldn't leave his dog," said William and, when Roach appeared to hesitate, he continued "I can take you there now if you've the time."

Roach looked questioningly at George who said:

"You go, Roach, but I'd best get back. Emma will be worried if I'm much later."

It was a good walk to the poacher's: along Church Road, across the fields and so to Butley Low Corner. A solitary light burned in the cottage, which was one of several situated on the lane. William gave a peremptory tap or two on the low door and entered without being asked. Harry Cole sat by the fireplace, his eyes fixed on a terrier that lay at his feet as still as the dead. The poacher started when he saw Roach but relaxed when William waved his hand in a reassuring manner.

"Mr Roach has been into the forest tonight, Harry. Have a word or two with him."

"I don't want to talk about it. I've nothing to say."

Roach ignored him and approached the terrier, kneeling by the dog's side on the mat.

"He's a Cairn, isn't he?" asked Roach, "He looks as though he's had a fit. That's unusual in the breed. They're very stable little dogs as a rule."

Roach's concern was enough to open Harry's mouth.

"You'd have had a fit if you'd seen what he saw last night."

"He's been like this all day?"

"I had to carry him home."

"Tell Mr Roach about what you saw, Harry. It'll clear your head – get it out of yourself."

"It'll help this little chap, too, Mr Cole. He's picking up on your tension. A fit doesn't last this long," said Roach, quietly, when the poacher hesitated; and all the while, Roach's hand never stopped stroking the terrier.

Harry Cole's eyes darted about the room, seeking doors and the one window as though he feared that there were listeners outside the walls; and then he relaxed, sank back into the wooden armchair and began to talk.

"We were out after ... rabbits – him and me, over by Staverton Park when we saw it coming. It weren't the first we'd seen but it were lower in the sky than the others and travelling slower. They're unnerving things, Mr Roach, I'll tell you, and when they're that close – jest above you – you wonder what's goin' to happen. I suppose I had those little children in mind – poor, little mites – and I was scared they'd come for me. I can face a keeper. I can stare down the barrels of his shotgun, but I wouldn't say thank you to see them again – not in a million years. Poor little Reggie went nuts – round and round in circles he ran, frothing at the mouth and yelping something terrible. He ain't a noisy dog by no means. He's a quiet little chap as a rule but that thing scared the living daylights out of him."

Harry paused, looked up at William and then across at Roach and the terrier, which was watching his master's turbulence and shaking from head to foot.

"Take it calmly, Mr Cole. Better out than in, as Mr Ward says," urged Roach, turning the terrier on its side and rubbing its chest in a slow, gentle movement.

"I've seen them, you see – and so's he – but not last night. Last night it was jest the flying ... thing. Lower and lower it came and I knew it were going to crash. There was no help for it. Straight into the forest it went. I heard the trees rend and tear as it tore into them. It's their speed that's frightening, and the way they turn so sudden. One minute it were racing at the forest and the next it were shooting skywards. No normal aircraft can behave like that – not with that suddenness ... but it came down, wobbling as though it were injured – like some animal."

"What did this thing look like, Mr Cole," asked Roach, daring to interrupt.

"It was circular and had what looked like a bun on top and below. I saw it. It was only a few hundred yards away. There were portholes along the upper part, and a thing that looked like a hatch on top ... Can I get you gents a drink?"

Harry Cole rose from the chair and went to a triangular-shaped cupboard that nestled in the corner of his living room, emerging with a bottle of port and some tumblers.

"Port's all I have. Left over from Christmas," he said with a smile.

"Port sounds good to me, Mr Cole," answered Roach as he took his glass, clinked it against his companions and took the first long sip. "It's not surprising that you're shaken, Mr Cole. As Mr Ward says, it's best to get these things out. Is there anything else you can tell me?"

"No – not now. Come back, perhaps, another time."

"Did you see the Americans arrive?"

"No, we left – Reggie and me," replied Harry, looking down at his dog and visibly more relaxed now that his fear was out in the open.

Roach and William Ward sat with Harry for a long time and talked of other matters and of nothing at all, but the company was good for Harry and for his Cairn terrier. Reggie was on his feet once the men seemed content in each other's company and once Harry had off-loaded his fears onto Roach. The little dog was soon wagging its tail and wanting food, which Harry chopped up in the kitchen and offered him on the fireplace mat.

As they walked, quite purposefully, back to the village neither man said much. Roach was no doubt wondering what else it was that Harry had seen. He'd mentioned seeing the disc-shaped things before and also "them" – whatever 'them' might be. A secretive man was the poacher: seeing 'them' was not the same as being seen by 'them'.

CHAPTER 4

Incident at the USAF Base

(Roach was not to become aware of the events related in this chapter until much later, as his diary indicates, but in the interests of clarity I felt it best to relate them here in their proper time and sequence.)

During the night of July 14, 1955 a security patrol at the RAF Bentwaters Base – which at that time, together with RAF Woodbridge, was part of the large USAF complex – saw unusual lights in the sky. These seem to fall into Rendlesham Forest. Fearing that one of their aircraft had crashed-landed, three of the USAF patrol obtained permission to enter the forest and investigate.

Upon reaching a clearing about a half a mile north of the eastern gate of the base's runway, the three men came upon a strange aircraft. It was circular in shape and about forty-five feet in diameter. On top and below the craft there was a dome, and a series of lights were spaced along the outer rim; these glowed quite steadily. As they watched, the whole structure seemed to pulse and discharge a low, disturbing whine. A strong, white light was emitted from the lower dome and this illuminated the ground below the craft. They could not tell whether the craft was hovering or whether it was supported by some form of landing gear.

Finding that their radio was inoperable within the deep enclosure of the pines, the three men immediately retreated to the edge of the forest where they communicated with RAF Woodbridge's security desk. The duty servicemen contacted

Suffolk police and two British police officers were dispatched to the forest to investigate.

PC Heath, who was 27 years old, later filed his report in which he stated that on their arrival at the clearing the two officers were startled to see 'a disc-shaped craft that gave off a grey-green glow. It was hovering about twenty-five feet above the ground and there were signs of some activity between the craft and the forest floor'. PC Heath was not specific about the nature of this activity but he concluded that 'figures were moving about in the strange glow and appeared to be undertaking some kind of work on the craft itself'. The craft was 'motionless' and neither officer felt that it was 'rotating'. PC Heath's report went on to say that 'there is no doubt that the craft we saw was a solid object. We did not notice any vents or portholes but concluded that the green glow came from the actual body of the craft'. On his return to Woodbridge he reported what he and his fellow constable had seen to a senior officer and then wrote his report, which both PCs signed.

Records show that the local radar stations at RAF Bentwaters and RAF Lakenheath, which is forty miles to the north, both recorded unexplained blips on their screens over the course of that night. RAF Lakenheath alerted RAF Neatishead on the Norfolk Broads. The RAF Chief Controller at Neatishead confirmed the sighting of what he described as 'an unidentified object at a height of about 15,000 feet and travelling at a tremendous speed. Its behaviour was erratic. It seemed to be able to stop suddenly and then accelerate from a stationary position. This is a feat that would be quite impossible for any aircraft I have seen on radar before'.

The verbal report of the two constables was communicated to Lieutenant Colonel Pat Humphreys, who was Deputy Base Commander, and he immediately organised a team to accompany him into the forest armed with Geiger counters and tape recorders. As they approached the clearing, Humphreys recalls hearing "very strange sounds and a light moving some way ahead". He remembers a feeling of nausea overwhelming him, and immediately brought his team to a halt. One of his men then pointed out a small, red light moving among the pine trees. It was described in his report as 'a red, sun-like light that pulsated and threw off bright, glowing shards of an intensity I have never experienced in any torch or lantern. One thing was certain. The light was coming our way'. Humphreys was about to call for reinforcements when he and his team were surrounded by a blinding, silent flash of light and everything was sucked upwards towards the light. The servicemen were thrown to the ground and their equipment scattered far and wide. Lieutenant Colonel Humphreys recalls striking a tree and supposes he must have lost consciousness because when he recovered he found his companions prone on the ground. He 'ascertained that they were still alive and able to go on', and then led his team towards the clearing only to find nothing there except the shattered trees. Without their torches, an effective search was impossible and so they returned to base where Humphreys made first a verbal and then a written report to the RAF base commander, Squadron Leader Douglas Fern.

The whole of Rendlesham Forest was cordoned off to prevent public access and during the following day a thorough search was made of the clearing and the immediate surrounding area. The scattered equipment was recovered and levels of radiation were found to be high; otherwise, apart from the broken pines, there was no suggestion that any craft had occupied the clearing during the previous night. There was no wreckage and no sign of a heavy craft having rested on the ground. Investigations continued under arc lights throughout the following evening, and it was at this time that Roach and George arrived to first annoy the sentry and then the implacable Lieutenant Colonel Pat Humphreys.

CHAPTER 5

Bird's Farm

Roach, once again, rose early and made his way to the toilet at the back of one of the cottages. He supposed that when the fishing families lived there they must have shared the one toilet; now, at least, it was only used by George, Emma and – for the summer – himself. He'd got into the habit on his first morning of emptying the waste, and so he trudged with the iron bucket to a spot as far from the cottage as possible, dug a hole and tipped in the previous day's excrement. He thought to himself that even in Sharjah it had not been this primitive. Still the rhubarb would be good!

Having heated the water on the kitchen stove and carried it in the enamel jug to the bowl in his room, Roach strip-washed, penned a note and left Creek Cottage quietly. He felt bad at leaving undone the work he had promised to carry out for Emma and George but he wanted to catch the poacher before he might be off for the day. He had no wish to harass the man, but he was concerned about the terrier.

Harry Cole was in his garden, swallowing the last gulps of a mug of tea and the Cairn was running around, having forgotten his terror of the day before.

"Morning, Mr Cole. Reggie's fine then?"

"Yes, you could say that if you liked."

It was obvious that the poacher had shaken off the tremors of the previous day and returned to his truculent mood, and so Roach made no attempt to ask the questions to which he needed answers.

"I won't trouble you further, Mr Cole, but if you would point me in the direction of someone who might be able to sort out this mystery I'd be grateful."

Roach had discovered as a child that if you made an adult's uselessness clear to them they would often be helpful: mortification was a great weapon. The poacher gave him a sideways glance and might have winced. Roach wasn't sure, but an answer came in grunted tones.

"See Jack Stevens. He knows."

The village bobby was on duty twenty-four hours a day. His job was his pride and joy; his 'patch' was crime free, and Roach found the house easily enough once a local had pointed the way. Jack Stevens welcomed Roach with a smile and offered him a cup of tea for which Roach was grateful since he had skipped breakfast that morning.

"You've missed breakfast! Come, come, what are Emma and George thinking of?"

"It was my fault. I left early. I wanted to see Harry Cole."

"Is he feeling better yet?"

"Is he usually off-hand?"

"Always, but he'll talk eventually. He likes to gather a crowd first. Doesn't like anyone else stealing his thunder," replied Jack with a smile, "I'm about to have breakfast, Mr Roach, and I'd be pleased if you'd share it with me."

While the policeman proceeded to cook what he called "a proper breakfast" – two sausages, two fried eggs, tomatoes, mushrooms and fried bread – Roach sat at the immaculately scrubbed kitchen table and listened.

"Being a country bobby has its compensations, Mr Roach. The ration applies out here but not in quite the same way as it might in the town ... I heard you'd been ejected from the forest by our American cousins, and I expect being an RAF man you'd like to know what's going on, wouldn't you?"

When Roach didn't reply, Jack Stevens continued:

"Two of our boys went into the forest ahead of the Americans and they saw what the papers refer to as a flying

saucer – not that the papers have got hold of this story ..."
Again he paused, and this time Roach urged him on, giving the
impression to the policeman that he was quite familiar with
the phenomena.

"Yes," he replied, casually, "Our radar stations have picked
them up all over Europe: Sweden, Norway, Finland and
Germany to mention but a few countries. During the war, we
thought they were German rockets. Later, they were taken for
some advanced Russian weapons. But no one was sure.
They've been called 'ghost rockets' and 'spook bombs'. They
are sometimes described as cigar-shaped and, at others, as
circular. They can emit bright lights and a whining sound or
fly silently."

"You seem to know more about it than I do, Mr Roach."

"No, no! Go on."

"The one our two boys saw was disc-shaped and gave off a
green glow. It was hovering above the ground, they said, and
something was going on around it."

"Like what?"

"Colin wasn't sure, but he swore there were figures moving
in the light. Once he'd made his report, the Americans took
over."

"Has there been any similar activity around here in the
past?" asked Roach.

"When we've had breakfast, I'll take you to see John Bird.
He runs a farm to the side of the forest and ... Here, let's eat."

It was the largest breakfast Roach had enjoyed since
arriving in Civvy Street and he wolfed it down. When they had
finished, Jack Stevens went next door to borrow his neighbour's
bike for Roach. Bird's farm was south of the village and east of
Tangham Walks.

"A distance of a couple of miles or so," he explained,
"Never walk if you can cycle and never cycle if you can ride."

Roach laughed at the policeman's country wisdom. They
mounted their bikes and within ten minutes were approaching
Bird's Farm.

"I've come," explained Jack, quietly, "because John Bird can be a funny bugger, and he's more likely to talk if I'm here."

John Bird did talk, but reluctantly. As the man went over his son's 'fall' down the stairs and his 'friend' in the forest, it was clear even to Roach, who lacked the policeman's experience of hesitant witnesses, that the farmer was holding back. When pushed, he first nudged their attention in the direction of Harry Cole and then exploded:

"I've told you, Jack, in confidence. I ain't having no report made. They'll think I'm a crackpot and I'll find myself locked up in St David's."

St David's was the local mental hospital: a place that engendered fear and loathing.

"I'm not an official investigator, Mr Bird," explained Roach, "I shall make no report about what you have to say, but you don't want your cows startled night after night and two children are missing."

"What's that got to do with it?"

"Perhaps nothing, but it might just be worth taking a look. Anything you have to tell me may be of some help."

"I've told PC Stevens."

"But in confidence, and he wouldn't pass it on without your permission. Besides, it always comes truer from the horse's mouth."

I have said that Roach was an amiable chap; he got on well with people, and John Bird sensed that here was someone he might trust.

"All right, but once I start don't stop me – and we'd best go out to the cowshed. It's quieter, and it won't trouble the wife."

The smell of the cowshed took Roach back to his childhood and his grandfather's job as a farm labourer. John Bird clearly felt at home there and his whole demeanour relaxed, even when Roach did interrupt his flow to ask a question.

"I was out one morning about to milk the cows. It was about eighteen months ago, and it was just before the sun came up. Suddenly, I heard this explosion. It was like a blast of wind, and I could swear that just before it happened there were lights in the sky. Well, I went to investigate and, blast me, if there wasn't a bloody great hole up there on the top field. The cows were all over the place and so I didn't stay long. I settled them down, did the milking and then, later in the day, I went back to look at this hole."

"How large was it?" asked Roach.

"It was about four feet across and three feet deep. I cycled down to get Jack and he had the army here in one-one-two. We thought it was a bomb at first but they couldn't find anything – only everything around the centre hole had been crushed: stones, crops, the lot. After a while other government experts turned up and began poking around with some kind of detector ..."

"A gradiometer," explained Jack Stevens.

"And that began to screech something terrible. The needle was jerking about all over the place. They dug down, and it was bloody hard work I can tell you, but they found nothing. Not a sausage."

"The detector indicated that there was a large metal object buried deep below the ground, but after a while the army gave up," said Jack Stevens.

"How far down did they probe?" asked Roach.

"Perhaps a hundred feet or more," he replied.

The three men looked at each other in silence. After a while, John Bird continued.

"The thing is, Mr Roach, nothing grows there. For about twenty-four feet round where that hole was nothing will grow. You've got good crops all around – potatoes on one side, barley on the other but nothing near that hole."

"A bomb could have detonated beneath the surface, Mr Bird, or maybe a meteorite landed. It would have hit the ground with enough force to drive it well underground," suggested Roach, reassuringly.

"That's what the army concluded," said Jack, and he and John Bird exchanged glances.

"Go on," urged Roach.

"A while after that happened I was out fishing on the Butley River with one of my farmhands ..."

Roach could see John Bird's pause indicated a struggle to speak that went beyond a mere search for the right word. The farmer rose and went to the door, leaning for a while on the jamb and gazing out over his fields. He closed the lower half of the door and leaned on it, reluctant to continue. Fearing the man might leave off his story altogether, Roach remained intensely silent, not daring to disturb the atmosphere in the cowshed. Eventually, the farmer returned and sat close beside the policeman on the hay bale. Had Roach not supposed otherwise, he might have assumed the farmer had been crying.

"We were on the river, you understand? There was no way that these creatures could have reached us ... but they must have done. I can't tell you exactly what they looked like because they seemed to keep changing shape ... They floated, see – or seemed to. I don't remember much, but they were about four feet tall whatever they looked like ... I think I must have fainted ... My farmhand, Dick Stevens ..."

"My cousin," explained Jack.

"He said they took us inside some craft or other ... and we were scanned by a device that had an eye. They smeared us with a sticky substance and there was this smell of gas. They took blood samples ... and others ..."

Struggling against speaking at all, John Bird was now crying visibly, much to his embarrassment, but the policeman urged him on.

"They were found dumped on the river bank," said Jack, "Both of them were jabbering."

"So would you, Jack Stevens, if the like was to happen to you. I never felt like that before. I never came across anything like that before. To have those creatures touching you – their ... hands ... can you call them hands? ... doing things to you."

John Bird ran to the cowshed door and yanked it open, but Roach was upon him in a moment and he and the policeman led the farmer back into the shed.

"Calm down, Mr Bird," said Roach, comfortingly, "Thanks for telling me. It's all over now. We'll have a cup of your red tea ... and I bet your wife bakes Suffolk scones, doesn't she? Thanks for explaining. It's been a great help."

"It's all right, Mr Roach. I've been through this a hundred times or more over a cup of red tea, early in the morning. That right, Jack?"

"That's right, John."

"I'm a family man. I've got responsibilities. I hold on tight."

Back in the farmhouse kitchen with the range burning bright even on this hot summer's day, the three men sat around and tucked into the scones Amanda Bird had, indeed, made. They washed these down with mugs of the scalding hot tea and John Bird began to smile.

"A lot of nonsense, Mr Roach – is that what you think?"

"I wouldn't say that, Mr Bird," replied Roach, quietly, amazed at how both the farmer and the poacher almost disowned their terrors once they were out in the open.

"You need to finish, John. If Mr Roach knows about these things, you need to let the boy tell him," said Amanda Bird.

John Bird looked reproachfully at his wife as though she was opening wounds he had tried so desperately to close.

"Only if the boy wants to tell me," suggested Roach – again with that quiet reassurance he possessed.

Norman Bird did want to tell Roach. He seemed eager to do so and it enabled him to have more than his fair share of scones as the story unwound.

"I was playing out with my friends and this boy joined us. He wasn't from the village 'cause he didn't go to our school, but he was all right. His clothes were different, but not posh or anything. They were just ... different."

"How different?" asked Roach.

"Well they were ... light ... they didn't seem to weigh nothing."

"You held this boy's clothes?"

"We were playing It and I grabbed at his jacket and it was so light it wasn't there."

"Go on."

"After a bit, he took me off with him. He held my hand and we sort of floated away ... the next morning I was in bed and he came to see me in my bedroom. He had a friend with him. I could hear Mum downstairs. She always brings some of that cod liver oil up to me with a glass of squash to wash it down."

"It's best to get it down so that he can enjoy his breakfast," explained Amanda.

"My friends skipped across the room and that made me laugh. They wanted to play. When Mum came in they hid behind the door and I could see them peeping out and laughing. Mum didn't know they were there and they kept making faces behind her back. When she'd gone, they came over to the bed and looked at me ... They didn't seem to want to play then but just ... look ... and ..."

"OK," soothed Roach, "On the day you fell down stairs and your Dad caught you, were these friends with you then?"

"How did you know?" asked Norman, looking at Roach as though he was a magician. "Yes, one of them had been with me in the bedroom and I ran out and tripped and Dad caught me."

"You floated down the stairs just as you floated away with your friend when you played together?"

"He wasn't with me. He just ... helped me float."

"Did you like your friend?" asked Roach.

The boy looked at him, resentfully, as though Roach had invaded his mind and disturbed a thought best kept quiet.

"I liked him," replied Norman, "but he frightened me."

"There, there, it's best out," said Amanda.

"Right, Mrs Bird. Best out. Thank you, Norman. Thank you, Mr Bird. I'm very grateful. You're quite right to forget about these things. Put them behind you. Enjoy your holidays, Norman. You break up soon, don't you?"

"Next week," replied the boy.

"Can you make head or tail of it, Mr Roach?" asked the farmer, as he escorted them to the farm gate.

"Not yet, Mr Bird, but we will, we will. Bye for now – and thanks again."

"Can you make head or tail of it?" asked Jack Stevens as they cycled south along the Capel Road.

"No. The hole is most likely to have been a bomb exploding beneath the ground – there are plenty of unexploded bombs along this coastline – and I imagine they took a bit to drink with them on the fishing trip, didn't they? As far as the boy is concerned – didn't you have an invisible friend when you were a child? I did."

Jack Stevens laughed.

"The only thing that really disturbed me was Mr Bird's obvious terror," continued Roach, "He was genuinely nauseated by the memory. At one time – perhaps even now – he must have been on the verge of a nervous breakdown. What caused that in what I assume is a steady man?"

"There's someone else I want you to see," said the policeman, suddenly, as thought he had just made up his mind on the matter. "That's why we're cycling away from the village. He's a forester. The pine plantations around here belong to the Forestry Commission and Steve Lomax works for them. He'll be in the area called Tangham Forest today."

"You keep your ear to the ground, Constable Stevens!"

"No villains on my patch, Mr Roach."

Steve Lomax was working in Tangham Forest and he looked up with a smile when Roach and the policeman rode into view. Suggesting it was time for elevenses, he poured them each a cup of coffee from a huge flask. The sun was quite high over the trees by this time, and the three men sat in the speckled light, content in each other's company, content to remain quiet and listen to the odd sounds of the forest: a few magpies, squirrels and the odd family of deer.

When Jack Stevens finally announced the reason for their visit, Steve Lomax frowned and suggested that Roach should read the report he had given the policeman. Stevens suggested that a story told is better than a story read and that "besides, Mr Roach may have some questions that only you can answer". The forester grinned.

"It's a grim tale, Mr Roach, and I don't dwell on it. These things are best shoved out of sight. I made my report and that's it, but for Jack's sake I'll go over it again for you. From the Ministry are you?"

"No. I got involved through Harry Cole and his Cairn terrier."

The forester laughed again.

"The only villain Jack tolerates! Is that right, Jack?"

"Harry Cole will meet his match, one day. I'll leave him to the keepers."

"Me and my mate had just packed up for the day. It was about a couple of years ago and we were marking up a new section of the forest for planting. We were heading home in the truck when we saw this glow among the trees. I told John to stop, and I'd go and take a look. When I got into the forest I saw this aircraft hovering over a clearing. It was making a beeping sound and spinning – like a kid's spinning top, really, I suppose. I've never seen anything like it before or since. I ran towards it. I thought it was some form of new-fangled aircraft these Americans were testing out, and I didn't want the forest set ablaze. I began to yell, hoping to attract their attention. There had to be somebody in the thing. Suddenly, I was hit by this beam of bright light and that's all I remember.

My mate must have driven off and then returned for me because he said that when he got back I was gone. When I woke up some time later, I was lying in a bunker on Bromeswell golf course. A golfer found me. I was dazed, he said, and so he took me to the inn at Bromeswell. I knew the landlord there and he had a car, and so he took me home."

Roach sensed that the forester was easing himself into a story that lacked the humour of having been found, apparently sozzled, in a bunker on the local golf course.

"I live with my sister. I'm not married. You know what women are like: she wormed the story out of me and insisted I told Jack ... I woke up after the light had hit me in a low, white room. It was very cool. Three creatures were standing round me. At first I thought they were insects, but when I yelled they seemed more human. They didn't like my yelling and they didn't like it when I clobbered them one. It was funny but hitting them was like thumping canvas. I jumped off the table I was lying on and ran out of the room.

And then the strangest thing of all – I ran straight into a human being. He was wearing a helmet like them ones Dan Dare wears, but he was human. I swear it. He took me by the elbows – I felt his hands – and he led me out of this aircraft. There was a slope. We walked down it and there were three more of these aircraft in front of us. We seemed to be in some sort of hangar. And standing by these aircraft were more men like you and me – all in these one-piece boiler suits, but not wearing helmets. They looked up as we came down, and then a mask was clamped over my face. It was like those gas masks they used to put you to sleep at the school dentists. When I came round, I was in the bunker."

Steve Lomax laughed, offered them another cup of coffee, which Roach and Jack Stevens refused because they didn't want to leave the forester short for the day, and then the talk drifted into matters of the village and the forest. Roach recorded in his diary that the forester seemed unaffected by his experience, preferring to forget what had happened and get on with his life. Cycling home, he asked Jack Stevens what had become of his reports.

"I was interviewed by the usual men in grey suits and told to keep the matter to myself since gossip could only spread

panic. Under no circumstances was I to go to the newspapers
– something I wouldn't have dreamed of doing, anyway,
Roach – and I was to advise the Birds and Steve Lomax to put
the matter out of their minds."

"The 'men in grey suits' – were they English or American?"

"One was a Scot and the other two were English with cut
glass accents."

CHAPTER 6

Harvest Time

And quiet the matter became: Roach noted with amazement that the day to day business of living overtook all that had happened, and almost overtook the disappearance of the Hargreaves children. Within two weeks, the school holidays had begun and so had the harvest. During that time, Roach woke early each morning and put a solid day's work into Creek Cottage. He and George drilled in a chemical damp course, concreted the floors and plastered those walls that would not "look nice as brick alone", which was the manner in which Emma expressed her dissatisfaction when they suggested leaving them unadorned. The day they came to look at the woodwork, the two men found that the rafters were free of worm and the roof tiles more or less intact.

"That just leaves the windows, floors and doors," said Roach.

"And the money to do the work," replied George with a wry laugh.

"I may be able to help there," suggested Roach, "As you know, my dad was a carpenter and I know one or two blokes in the timber business. William Brown's in Ipswich may be able to help us out."

Forty years later, George remembered Roach's kindly half-lie with gratitude. His father had been a carpenter and he did know "one or two blokes in the timber business", but what he didn't mention was that he was well off, having had nothing to spend his money on in the forces, and fully intended to pay for the wood himself.

"Well, if you can get us a deal, Dave, we'd appreciate it," was what he said at the time before continuing "but not today or tomorrow. It's traditional to help out with the harvest and Bird has a field of barley that needs gathering in. We may as well take a couple of stout sticks with us in case we're lucky enough to flush out a few rabbits – and we will be!"

Roach was familiar with the traditions of the harvest from the time he had spent with his grandfather, and he had an enormous respect for the work of farmers and farm labourers. They brought the country through the war. They laboured long hours, often in freezing weather with filthy mud in every yard. It was a seven day a week job from six in the morning to six at night most of the time. During the harvest they worked until they could see no longer. But there were the joys, too, and harvest time was one of them.

As the combine worked its way round the field dropping off the bales of straw, it was a pure thrill to catch them up on the end of your pitchfork or pass them along a chain of hands and watch the haystack rise from the ground. There was plenty of labour: apart from the usual farm workers, gypsies would turn up and villagers would turn out. The summer of '55 was a glorious one and sweat ran freely from mid-morning, but there was always a flagon or more of cider waiting in the cool of a hedge to quench your thirst and drive you on.

William Ward had brought his two children along, and Rachel and Tom sat upon the stack as it rose. Roach knew what would happen: as soon as it was too high to reach, ladders would be placed against the sides so that the men could place the bales accurately, and then they would remove the ladders and leave the youngsters stranded high on the haystack. It was great fun up there – another world where you romped in the straw.

By lunchtime, a goodly part of the field was harvested and Roach sat with the Wards and George to eat the sandwiches Emma and Agnes had prepared and drink John Bird's cider or, in the case of the children, Agnes's lemonade.

During the physical labour of the past two weeks, Roach had pondered on the tales he heard; indeed, it was at this time he began to keep his diary. It was easy to dismiss Norman Bird's account of his 'friends' as a child's imagination and credit John Bird's to drink, but Roach was less ready to disregard Steve Lomax's strange tale of his apparent abduction and the human beings in space helmets and boiler suits. He also found it difficult to shake off the sight of the little dog trembling in Harry Cole's hearth and the poacher's terror.

"You've heard no news of your friends, I take it?" he asked, turning to Tom and Rachel.

"No, Mr Roach. They haven't come back," replied Rachel.

"But we haven't been up to the big house, and so we don't know," continued Tom.

"Nor will you," said William quietly.

"Are you concerned for their safety, Mr Ward?" Roach asked.

"It's best to keep away from strange goings-on, Mr Roach, if you see what I mean."

Roach understood the last phrase to indicate that he should drop the conversation, which he was reluctant to do. As it was, Tom's intervention avoided the need to offend the children's father.

"We think they went for a ride in the spaceship."

"What are you talking about?" snapped William.

"The spaceship that Mr Cole saw land in the forest," replied Rachel, defending her brother.

"How'd you know about that?"

"Everyone knows, Dad. All the children at school were talking about it."

"It's hard to keep gossip quiet, Mr Ward," laughed Roach, thinking it was time he sought out Harry Cole for the rest of what he had to say.

"Ah," replied William, "The Devil makes work for idle hands and gossip for idle tongues."

His voice bore the tone of mock disapproval, and this only egged the children on.

"Sir Robert has drawings of spaceships in his study," said Tom, "Perhaps it was one of his."

"How do you know that? You haven't been in his study, have you?" asked William, anxiously.

Rachel was quelled by her father's tone but emboldened by Roach's wink.

"We were playing with Patricia and Myles last summer. We were on the terrace and saw Sir Robert go off with his shotgun. We weren't supposed to go in his study but Myles and Patricia wanted to and the window was open and so we peeped in ... Patricia said it would be all right ..."

"Go on," said William, "You've started. You may as well finish."

"Their dad keeps all his important papers in a secret compartment in his desk drawer, and Myles and Patricia had never seen in there, but when we looked the papers were all over his desk ... and so we went in and there were drawings of spaceships like Tom said."

"What did they look like?" asked Roach, "If I give you a piece of paper could you draw one for me?" he continued, tearing off a piece of greaseproof paper in which Emma had wrapped his sandwiches. "You don't mind, do you, Mr Ward?"

Rachel and Tom looked at their father as they took the scraps of paper from Roach. William grunted and reached in his pocket for a pencil. Roach provided a second one and watched as the children drew. Neither looked up at the other nor made any attempt to see what their sibling was drawing, so intent was each child on their work. Rachel's spaceship (although George was loath to suppose that it was anything of the sort) was circular with a dome above and below. It had what appeared to be three legs protruding from the base of the craft and a row of windows in the top dome. Tom's was similar but with neither legs nor windows.

"How would you get out of that one, Tom?" asked his father with a laugh.

"There was a ladder," replied the boy, "I haven't finished the drawing yet."

Roach smiled to himself. "How easy it is to be taken in!" he said later to George. Roach simply couldn't imagine any advanced 'creatures' – and advanced they must be to produce such aircraft – needing a ladder to exit their vehicle. *If Sir Robert had been doodling idly, he hadn't shown much imagination* is what Roach wrote in his diary that evening.

"Is Sir Robert involved in aircraft design?" he asked.

"I've no idea where he works," replied George, "Have you, Mr Ward?"

"Can't help you," replied William, "All I know is he works up in London. But he'll be along this afternoon. This is his field. John Bird farms it for him but he owns it, and he always likes to see how things are doing. And then, of course, there's the rabbits just waiting for the pot."

The idea of rabbits 'waiting for the pot' wasn't one that appealed to Roach, but he knew what William Ward meant. During the war, rabbits had been an essential source of meat for everyone – townsfolk included: they were (as the wartime poster explained) 'off the ration'. All morning the animals had been scuttling further and further towards the heart of the barley field, but soon there would be nowhere to crouch in hiding. As the last standing stalks fell they would have to bolt for cover to the nearest hedgerow. As they ran, shotguns would pick them off and beaters would be waiting by the hedges with heavy sticks ready to club them to death or chase them out towards the guns. Roach had no objection to shooting a single rabbit for dinner – meat had only been off the ration since '54 and old habits die hard – but the terror involved in this mass slaughter turned his stomach.

"We'd best get on," continued William, "We might even finish early this evening."

They rose and returned to their work. As the grain was sacked and the bales were stored, Roach kept an eye out for Sir Robert's arrival. When the landowner did appear, he came with a twelve bore shotgun under one arm. His practised eye swept the field and the workers with the skill of one used to sizing up his men. Roach discovered later that he had been in the RAF during the war, had risen to the rank of Wing Commander and would certainly have been made a Group Captain had he not insisted on remaining in what he termed "active service".

He sought Roach out immediately as the stranger, and engaged him in conversation. His handshake was firm and "daunting", as Roach later explained it to George.

"I understand you took an interest in our little accident the other day, Mr Roach?"

Quite used to service understatement and the beginnings of a dressing down, Roach smiled and replied:

"The crash landing, you mean? Yes, Sir Robert, it did *interest* me, as you say. I was in the RAF ..."

"Yes, I know: Eastleigh in East Africa and Sharjah on the Persian Gulf. I believe you were camp photographer at Sharjah – apart, of course, from your wireless operator duties."

"Yes, Sir Robert, I did take an interest in photography."

"You ran the camera club and took the official photographs, including any crashes, I believe?"

"There weren't many of those, sir," replied Roach, regretting his drop into respect for a senior officer the moment he uttered the word 'sir'."

"So I gather. You wouldn't by any chance have a camera standing by, would you?"

"No, sir – Sir Robert – I don't have a camera of my own."

"We'll see if we can put that matter right, Mr Roach. It would be a shame to see a talent go to waste."

Roach was feeling more than bulldozed by the conversation when a shout went up and the first group of rabbits made their dash for freedom. Sir Robert's gun, which he had held in the broken position, was on his shoulder so quickly that Roach couldn't believe it possible. Both barrels discharged and two rabbits were jerked in the air by their death throes before slumping back among the stubble. Before Roach had time to offer to fetch Sir Robert's kill, the landowner had ejected the empty cartridges, reloaded and fired off two more shots. The second pair of rabbits dropped not more than a hundred yards from the first.

Aware that several pairs of eyes were upon him from among the farmworkers and the gypsies, Sir Robert smiled.

"I've been shooting since I was a boy," he explained with a laugh.

"So have I," replied Roach, "but not quite with that turn of speed."

"In that case, Mr Roach, please borrow my gun."

"I'm more used to a 410."

"This has a greater kick, but hold it firmly into your shoulder and you'll not notice too much of a difference," Sir Robert replied with a smile and relishing the understatement.

Roach declined the offer. He broke company with Sir Robert to join Tom and Rachel at one of the hedges where they stood, a stout stick in their hands, waiting for the first unwary rabbit to attempt a dash for freedom. Roach, catching the eye of an occasional rabbit, withheld his blow and allowed it to escape.

"Hunting knits us together, Mr Roach," called Sir Robert, as the day's work drew to a close. The landowner stood, fourteen rabbits hanging from a branch he held across one shoulder. "It is essential to the social fabric of the countryside. Together, we find plenty of sport with which to fill the larder. Would you care to join me tomorrow? We might enjoy a rough shoot."

"Thank you", replied Roach, "I'd enjoy that very much"

"Mid-morning then? Now, if you'll excuse me, I'll drop these off on the way home. I expect there will be a few villagers glad of them tomorrow."

As they walked home, William Ward explained the traditions surrounding hunting and shooting.

"Most of the farmers around here are tenants, but the toffs aren't a bad lot. We beat for them during the pheasant season and they're quite happy for us to pot any number of rabbits or pigeons. They're considered vermin, and the landlords often supply the cartridges as a means of keeping the buggers under control. Mind you, they wouldn't be so keen on us bagging ourselves a pheasant or two – or even a grouse! I enjoy a shoot. Sometimes, I'll be out with a friend at dusk, just as the pigeons come home to roost. It's quiet at that time and they make good eating."

Later that evening, as they sat talking after the supper of cheese macaroni Emma had prepared, George mentioned the drawings made by the Ward children, having explained to Emma their similarity; and Roach shared with them Harry Cole's description of the aircraft the poacher had claimed to see crash-land in the forest.

"What do you make of it all, Dave?" asked Emma.

Roach acknowledged his reservations about the incidents surrounding John Bird and his children but indicated his reluctance to discount Steve Lomax's story.

"Who would the humans in the space suits be – even supposing the other ... beings were from ... outer space? The Americans can't be in league with ...," Emma asked, and then laughed at her own fancies, "Oh, this is ridiculous! It's like something my brothers used to read in the *Eagle*."

"Dan Dare and the Mekon, Lord of the Treens, who lived on Venus and was noted for his intellect and his flying chair, which he needed to carry his wasted body around and which he controlled with his mind. No, I think we can leave that to the children. Two things stand out for me: Steve Lomax's story and the children's drawings," replied Roach, "If the beings in the boiler suits and glass helmets were human, then they were presumably from Bentwaters ... unless Steve was taken further afield."

"The drawings the children saw in Sir Robert's study could just have been doodles, couldn't they?" suggested George.

"Of course – or they could have been designs for a new type of aircraft, and it could have been such a craft that crashed-landed in the forest. In which case, neither our government nor the Americans would have wanted it known."

"But how does all this link with the disappearance of the children?" asked Emma.

"I don't know that it does. Perhaps Sir Robert is right and they ..." Roach suddenly paused, frowned, opened his hands in the traditional gesture of helplessness and then continued, his voice laced with amazement, "Do you know it's just occurred to me. He never mentioned the children today – not once – and it never once occurred to me to ask ..."

"And yet it's more than two weeks since they disappeared," exclaimed Emma.

"Yes ... He's invited me to go shooting tomorrow. Perhaps I'll broach the matter when we meet. They may have turned up for all we know."

Later, as the two men strolled down to The Oyster, George said:

"You don't think our government is involved in this business, do you Roach?

"They may well be involved in the development of a new type of aircraft, George, but I hardly think they – or the Americans – would be in league with ... how do the science fiction stories put it? ... Oh yes, 'denizens of another world', replied Roach, drawing deeply on his briar, "No, I don't."

CHAPTER 7

Rough Shoot

Sir Robert was waiting and keen to talk to Roach when he arrived the next morning. They wandered, *almost aimlessly* Roach wrote in his diary, potting the odd rabbit and the occasional pheasant and grouse.

"Your cousin's wife will be pleased with the pheasants, Mr Roach. Have you plucked a bird before?"

"My grandfather taught me," replied Roach.

"Ah yes, you have the countryside in your blood. Let the bird hang for a while in the pantry to ripen, but only a day at the most. In this infernal heat, the meat will go off very quickly. There are many poor cottagers around here and they are only too glad of a rabbit, a hare or a pigeon – even a magpie or a jay. I shall get one of my men to distribute today's bag. Rabbits and pigeons are a confounded nuisance, as you might imagine. I have no objection, myself, to a farmworker taking the odd pheasant, but it isn't to be encouraged, of course. Have you met Mr Cole?"

"Yes," replied Roach, *somewhat uncertainly* he wrote later because he had no wish to get Harry Cole into trouble.

"My keeper sustains a weather eye on Mr Cole, since he profits from his thefts, but we wish him no harm."

Roach was aware that the conversation – or monologue, since Sir Robert had dominated their talk – had moved rapidly to the subject of Harry Cole or, more importantly thought Roach, to his role as the source of gossip surrounding the crash landing of the aircraft. Roach hesitated to respond, but felt himself unable to refrain.

"I did see Mr Cole the night of the crash landing," he said, "He was concerned for his dog."

"Naturally. He was quite close to the site, I believe?"

How Sir Robert could have supposed such information Roach was unaware, but denial would have led nowhere and so he said:

"Yes, he saw the craft as it crash landed."

"How did he describe it, Mr Roach?"

Again, Roach felt impelled to tell the truth, fight against it though he would, and he described the disc-shaped craft with its "bun on top and below" and its "portholes along the upper part, and a thing that looked like a hatch on top".

"What did you make of the poacher's description?"

"I rather thought he was imagining things in the dark of the night or that he was seeing an experimental aircraft that was being developed at RAF Bentwaters."

"Precisely. The Russians are a perceived threat, are they not? Either we develop such a craft or they do – and the winner of the race rules the skies?"

"I can't say I've really thought much about such matters. They are best left to the politicians."

"Come, come, Mr Roach, do you really believe such nonsense?"

"I have faith in my government."

"In what way and to what extent does your 'faith' embrace your government?"

"In that they will make the best decisions in the interests of the country."

Sir Robert raised his head and lifted it backwards before laughing. Roach's unease increased. Here was a man who – it was generally thought – worked for the government, and yet who was laughing at the idea it could be trusted.

"What is your philosophy of life, Mr Roach?"

Roach possessed no such philosophy. He had grown into adulthood believing that governments acted in the best interests of their people and that he – Roach – could be left to get on with his life in the sureness of that view.

"Politicians, Mr Roach, rarely know what decisions to make: that is left to the Civil Service who, it is supposed, understand such matters and offer their best advice – and they do! But we must ask ourselves whether or not that advice is flawed ... or, rather, whether that advice is as well informed as it might be ... We have recently emerged from a terrible war, and we must be sure of our leaders. We cannot be led back into such an inferno again – not in our lifetimes, not in our children's lifetimes!"

Roach was tired with all this talk (he had come out for a shoot, not a lecture), and yet he was fascinated and could do nothing but listen.

"Leaders are the key to our future. We must be certain to appoint the right leaders, and they will be the ones with the right philosophy ... You are familiar with Mr Darwin's theory, are you not – the belief that animal and plant life on this world evolves and that the evolution is decided by the need to survive?"

"Yes," replied Roach, unsure how the great naturalist's discoveries might be reflected in the ballot box.

Sir Robert looked at him, his lips pursed thoughtfully as though he was considering Roach for a job and assessing his worthiness.

"There are two opposing forces in our universe: the one urges us to continually create and diversify, while the other seeks to preserve the existing order and, by so doing, resist the force of life. Change is continuous and dynamic, not discrete and static. The force that encourages us to diversify is meandering: that is to say, it has no pre-ordained purpose. The future is determined not by some prior cause but by its potential for survival. We have seen how plants and animals have evolved from micro-organisms in the primeval swamp. This is the way of intuition and instinct, which is superior to that of intellect and reason."

The knight's eyes continued to stare at Roach as he spoke; they pierced into his mind to such an extent that Roach felt himself to be *in the presence of a madman*.

"Do you understand me?"

"No, I do not, Sir Robert," replied Roach, "You seem to be suggesting that we need leaders who would 'create and diversify' our lives rather than 'preserve the existing order'. I should have thought we had just fought a war against that very notion."

"The Fascists merely wished to replace one existing order with another of their own making. Had they won, the ability to diversify would have been eroded completely. There was no life force in the Nazis; they would have resisted change of any kind. We need leaders who possess the wisdom to embrace change, and thus ensure the survival of ... our species."

"I have always thought of instinct as belonging to the animal world, Sir Robert, and reason as being ..."

"Of a higher order? Of mankind?"

"Yes ... to act without reason is to deny our intellectual superiority to the animal world."

"We are animals, Mr Roach. To deny that fact is to deny the continuous flow of experience, it is to dissipate energy and resist the flow of life – and yes, we do need leaders who will recognise this simple truth."

Roach felt lost in a *mire of tautology*. Either this man was mad or he – Roach – was stupid, and something told him that the latter was not true. As he watched Sir Robert's shotgun being raised time and time again to the knight's shoulder, Roach wondered why the man had invited him to the rough shoot. What was his purpose in explaining such a bizarre view of life to a complete stranger?

"What are your future plans, Mr Roach?"

Roach explained that he thought his training as a wireless operator might secure him work with the BBC or that his interest in photography might open chances in that industry.

"How would you feel about working in the photographic department of the De Havilland Aircraft Corporation? You have some very relevant experience they might find very useful."

"That would be ideal, Sir Robert, but I am at a loss as to how I might approach such a company."

"I have interests in the Corporation, Mr Roach, and I will be pleased to put in a word on your behalf. Consider the matter settled. Finish your work here over the summer and report to the Corporation's HQ in Hertfordshire in September."

Roach was dumbfounded both by the knight's offer and the silence that followed. They continued the shoot until lunchtime, each occupied by his own thoughts: Sir Robert purposefully and Roach in a daze. When they sat for lunch on a hillock that overlooked Tunstall Forest, Roach was not surprised to see one of Sir Robert's men appear on horseback carrying a picnic basket. Nor was he surprised when the contents of the basket were revealed: herb pate with freshly baked bread, small mutton pies, fruity flapjacks and iced tea punch. *Apart from the bananas in the flapjack, there were no ingredients here that could not be garnered locally*, Roach wrote in his diary.

"I have an interest in these strange craft, Mr Roach, and you are clearly an intelligent young man. If you would keep your ear to the ground over the next few weeks and let me know about anything of interest you might learn, I should be grateful," Sir Robert said, as they tucked into the food his cook had prepared.

"One of my young pilots had a troubling experience during the war. We'd made a raid on Essen. We were bombing their steelworks along the Ruhr. His bombs dropped, my Flight Lieutenant turned his Lancaster for home. He'd no sooner done so than he received a message over the intercom. His rear-gunner reported that they were being followed by some odd looking lights.

They thought at first that the lights were flak or Luftwaffe night-fighters and the pilot tried to evade them. He manoeuvred his plane: dropping it out of the sky, standing it on its tail and making a series of corkscrews and turns in order to shake off whatever was in pursuit of our plane. But nothing would

66

throw them off. They were clearly tailing the Lancaster and they seemed to be able to accelerate in any direction they chose. As the bloody things closed in, the gunner reported them to be on either side of our plane almost simultaneously.

My pilot was unsure what to do. He didn't want order the gunner to fire in case that very action caused an explosion. He had the idea they might be some form of radio-controlled rocket devised by the Germans: their 'secret weapon' was much in the news at the time. This went on for ten minutes. Eventually, as the Lancaster flew over the Dutch coast, the lights just vanished.

My pilot reported it when they returned to base, which was RAF Mildenhall. I wouldn't have given the matter much credence – putting it down to strain and fatigue on the part of the crew – except that it wasn't an isolated event. After the war, I made a few enquiries and it turned out that these lights were seen by German night-fighter crews as well. Not only that but they were also seen in other parts of the world – Japan included."

"Did any aircrew fire at these lights?" asked Roach.

"One American crew did – somewhere over the Baltic – but they didn't return fire. They just vanished."

It was only when they said goodbye back at the hall that Roach felt able to broach the subject of the disappearance of Sir Robert's children.

"Thank you for enquiring, Mr Roach. It is reassuring, of course, that they have not been found, but I have no idea where they might be, and my dear wife is distraught with worry. They are public school children, of course – well able to fend for themselves in the English countryside, especially in summer when the pickings are ripe. They are used to standing on their own two feet and sleeping rough. Both are able to live off the land. They could catch and skin a young rabbit before you or I could blink. Sweet as a nut, you know – a young rabbit – and the skin comes off so cleanly. *Scouting for Boys* is a set text at Myles's school. But naturally, we are very worried and are pursuing all possible lines of enquiry."

Public schools are renowned for the independent spirit they inculcate in their pupils, but even so ... Roach wrote that night. He thought back to the freedom of his own childhood, and could just about understand Sir Robert's attitude, but even with his own experience he found it somewhat cavalier.

His diary entry about the children ends with the row of dots. He then goes on to say that he now understood Sir Robert's generosity. Roach was to *keep his ear to the ground and report back any odd occurrences with strange craft.* This seemed straightforward enough. After all, the knight was involved with a leading aircraft company and the post-war race was on to be the first country to develop a new type of aircraft: one that would be capable of rapid turns of speed and could travel with impunity through enemy radar.

Emma was less casual about Sir Robert's attitude towards his children when Roach mentioned it during supper.

"I suppose if your children are away at school most of the time that you get used to not seeing them around but ... I don't think I'd be so calm if, in the future, any of mine simply vanished into thin air."

"Like a tooth being extracted," mused George, "That's how young Ward described it."

"And it's over two weeks now. It was just before the children broke up for the summer. I can understand Sir Robert's wife being distraught. Did you meet her, Dave?"

"No," replied Roach.

"She's a very pleasant person. Sir Robert usually holds a fete on his land over the summer and his wife presides. I wonder if I should go and see her."

"That would be kind," said Roach, "God – if they were my kids, I'd give them hell when they got back. That's, of course, if I ever have any children."

"Oh, Dave, that reminds me. There's a telegram for you. I hope it's not bad news."

"It won't be," replied Roach, "It's from my father. I telegrammed him yesterday about the door and window frames ... He's only too pleased to give us a hand – or rather, have us give him a hand. He's a trained cabinet maker, you know. He served his apprenticeship at Tibbenhams in Ipswich. That's where he met my mother. She was an upholsteress. I've told him you've got no decent tools, George, and so he'll bring his own, and I see that Browns have dropped us off a carpenter's horse with the wood."

"Where will he sleep?" cried Emma.

"He can use my room. I'll manage. Don't get your knickers in a twist, Emma. Just woo him with your home cooking. He'll love that: a great trencherman is my Dad. In a couple of weeks, you'll have doors and windows. I'll go and meet him off the Woodbridge train tomorrow. I'm looking forward to another ride on Nathan Catchpole's bus."

CHAPTER 8

Encounters

The fortnight that Roach's father spent at Emma and George's Butley cottage went like wildfire, and by the time he left they had not only frames but also renovated doors and windows. The old man – I call him 'old' but, in reality, he was only in his late forties – charmed his way with Emma and, indeed, the rest of the village. Being a regular drinker at his own local, the Spread Eagle in Ipswich, he was soon ensconced, during the evenings, at the Butley Oyster.

It was here that he fell into regular conversation with Harry Cole. Like his son, Ernest Roach was an amiable man and being older and somewhat wiser in the ways of endearing himself to people he soon had the poacher "spilling the beans".

"You come along tonight, my boy," he said to Roach early on in the first week of his visit and you'll find out what it is troubling this place."

Ernest had settled himself with Harry in a corner seat where he could press his back tightly up against a settle and blow his pipe smoke out through a neighbouring window. Here, away from the ears of the rest of the bar, Harry sank his third pint, washed it down with his third whisky and began to talk without the gruff reservations he had shown towards Roach. There was no "come back tomorrow" in his manner under Ernest's twinkling eye; Roach's father was more friend than inquisitor.

"It's a hobby, you understand? It's not so much the odd few bob I might make from selling the odd game bird; it's more the

70

sport of it. I'm not one for the poaching gangs. I don't look for trouble. I don't manhandle the keepers."

Roach was about to ask how a keeper might be manhandled when he was silenced by the slight wave of his father's hand across the table. "Silence, my boy," he said later, "Be a good listener. Let the speaker ramble and tell the tale in his own way".

"I'd had a bit of trouble, though," Harry continued, unaware of Ernest's remonstrating hand, "Some of my nets had been found and a few snares; and the keeper up at the hall had warned me off. So on this particular night I was down on the edge of the forest after rabbits and I thought I might be lucky enough to find a grouse or two as well. I'd set some new snares the previous night and I weren't expecting any trouble. There's a deal of open grassland on the base and the rabbits seem to like the open spaces. It gives them warning of the foxes, you see.

It were a light night – thanks mainly to the moon being nearly full – but cloudy. So the light would come and go. If you've ever hunted on such a night, you'll know what I mean when I say the shadows can play tricks on your eyes. One minute the moon's out and the shadows are everywhere and the next you're in complete darkness when a cloud takes away the light.

I didn't have Reggie with me that night. I was in and out of the forest and he would have made a racket moving around. He's all right if you're after rabbits over the open field or looking for an otter along the creek, but Reggie ain't so handy in the forest. Anyway, I'm glad he weren't with me 'cause he would have yelped when he saw them. I don't know what they were up to. I ain't sure whether they came out of the base or were somewhere in the forest. The first I saw of them was when I looked up from checking a snare and glanced across a low hedge. I thought they were in some sort of armour, at first, but then I realised that was what they looked like ..."

He paused and gazed at his audience. Roach said he was exasperated but fascinated. Harry Cole was dragging the story, but he clearly wasn't out to impress. *It isn't that he hasn't got the imagination: being out at night on your own would soon take care of any lack in that quarter,* Roach wrote in his diary that night, *It's simply that Harry made no attempt to build up any tension in his telling. It was all so prosaic: details of snares and nets and Reggie's noisy movements but no attempt at creating a weird or ghostly picture.*

"If you can imagine something like a giant beetle or cockroach standing on its hind legs, you can picture what these things looked like. When they moved their heads to look about, their whole body turned, and instead of having hands like you and me they had these feelers on the end of their arms. Their backs were like the shell of a cockroach. That's what made me think they were wearing some kind of armour, but it weren't – it was them. I couldn't see their feet – not at first – because, like I say, they were walking along behind the hedge. I dursn't dare follow but after they'd gone by I stuck my head through a gap in the hedge and watched them walk on. I couldn't see their feet even then but their legs below the shell were thin. I could see that even in the dark."

"You said the other night that they were about four feet tall, Harry," said Ernest. "You reckon they were fully grown, do you? Adult?"

"As I said, they were about four feet high and about half as broad as you or me."

"Did they walk easily?"

"They sort of scuttled along, but upright. They didn't look as though they were about to fall over but they swayed a bit."

"But you didn't see their faces?" asked Roach, glancing at his father.

"I didn't say that ... It was while I was watching them go by that I became aware of another one. It must have been behind the others for some reason or other and when I turned my head to wriggle back through the hedge I happened to look up and saw it staring down at me. I don't know who was more surprised – it or me. But I got a quick look at its face. You've watched them great water beetles in a pond when you were a kid, haven't yer? Well, it weren't unlike one of them: a large mouth for grabbing its prey and eyes on short stalks. I pulled my head back quick, then, I can tell yer, and I was off like a shot."

Harry had little more to offer that night. On the way back to Creek Cottage, Roach said to his father and George:

"What do you make of his story?"

"Has he the imagination to make up such a tale – even to seek attention?" asked Ernest.

"I can well believe he might make up a tale. William Ward reckoned he liked an audience, and being at the centre of a mystery guarantees that people take notice of you. He claims to have seen these aircraft before. Would it take too much imagination to link the craft with some weird occupants?"

"I don't think Harry has ever been to the pictures in his life," said George, "That would involve a trip into town, and he rarely leaves his dog for too long. Besides – cockroaches and beetles? Have you ever heard of creatures from another world being described in that way? In the papers, they're usually 'little, green men" aren't they: spindly legs, big eyes, large heads?"

It was at that moment, listening to George the rational schoolmaster, that I began to feel insanity creeping in on me, wrote Roach.

The next morning, working alongside his father, Roach was glad to be driving nails through floorboards and into the joists of the upstairs rooms. The sheer, physical pleasure of clouting something hard with a large hammer seemed to reassure him. When Emma brought them coffee and some of her wonderful Suffolk scones for their elevenses and they sat resting their backs against the newly dried plaster of the bedroom walls, Roach said:

"Do you believe the poacher's story, Dad?"

"Is the man a liar or is he not? It's as simple as that, boy. Mind you, I can't say that I can make head or tail of it. That would take a keener brain than mine."

Roach wasn't sure of the 'liar or not' supposition. He was aware of the power of the imagination in everyone, however ruralised their lives might be. *Indeed*, he wrote, *it was from the countryside that all our folk tales originated. Where the hell did the stories of goblins, dwarfs, fairies and the like come from if not the human imagination?*

"Would you mind if I abandoned you this afternoon?" asked Emma when she came to collect their empty cups and plates, "I thought I might go and see Lady Hargreaves. Poor soul! She's a nice enough person, and she must be worried beyond belief at the moment. I will be back in time to cook our supper."

"And what may I ask will that be?" said Ernest.

"Wait and see," Emma laughed, "Oh, I don't think it will rain but I've got the washing on the line. Will you keep your eye on it?"

Neither Roach nor his father had ever kept their eye on washing in their lives but they both nodded sagely and gave each other a hopeful wink.

It is now difficult to appreciate the effort Emma had to make in approaching "the big house". During those post-war years, the old traditions of church-going and respect for your betters were a natural way of life. During the summer, when the Hargreaves family was in residence, Emma often saw Lady Hargreaves in church on a Sunday morning but they never spoke as a matter of course. The Hargreaves family had their own pew at the front of the church just below the pulpit: a position no one else would have dreamed of occupying. There was no snobbery involved: merely an acceptance of tradition – and, perhaps, a degree of thoughtlessness. Roach's generation was to challenge such assumptions, but not at that moment.

Emma did not resent these attitudes. The rural way of life with its landed gentry and church as key focal points provided the villagers with a sense of community within which everyone had a role. The bell ringing, the church jumble sales and the village fetes were all part of traditions that went back centuries. Only the elderly tugged their forelocks anymore should they meet a titled person or a gentleman farmer and their families – Roach's father's generation returning from the war had scuppered that mode of deference – but people were still keen to "keep up standards", and Emma was all for what was seen as "respectability". Talking in their cottage over forty years later, she told me of her trepidation on that day when she approached what was to her another world.

It therefore came as a shock that Lady Hargreaves welcomed her with almost open arms.

"She struck me immediately as a human being, and I'd never imagined her in that way. She was so gaunt with worry, she could have been my own mother when things got on top of her," said Emma, when she returned to Creek Cottage that evening.

"Has she no more idea of where her children might be than Sir Robert?" asked Ernest.

"Sir Robert was away – I don't know where but he'd been gone since early morning – and I think that not only was she glad of the company but that his absence gave her a freedom to speak."

Roach's diary noted the salient facts garnered by Emma, but it wasn't until I spoke to her that a complete picture of their meeting was made clear. Despite there being little more than a ten year difference in their ages, Emma said she felt very much younger than the knight's wife.

"Lady Hargreaves, I hope you won't consider this an intrusion ..." Emma began, only to be silenced by a gentle wave of the hand.

"Call me Geraldine, my dear. You are the schoolmaster's wife, are you not?"

"Yes. Emma Barber."

"Let us sit in the garden. I'll have some tea sent out. It's very kind of you to come – very kind. I suppose people are afraid to approach us, but we are human."

The tears came after a maid had brought the tea, together with a plate of blackberry muffins, and they had engaged in small talk for an acceptable period of time.

"I fear for the children and I fear for Robert," Geraldine Hargreaves said, replenishing Emma's cup for the second time, "He is a good man and I love him dearly but ... he has suffered some strange experiences, and I do wonder whether the war has disturbed him immeasurably."

Emma said that Lady Hargreaves glanced at her before continuing.

"Jack Stevens is very thorough, of course – an estimable young man – and I understand that your husband's cousin, Mr Roach, has taken an active interest in the strange happenings?"

"Yes," replied Emma, suspecting that her ladyship was on the edge of a confidence.

"Robert and I spend much of our time at the London house, of course, and the children are away at boarding school for most of the year. They are very attached to their school and I am sure they are safe ... Robert had taken me to Harrods on one occasion. It was our anniversary and he always consults when buying the present. It's always difficult for a decisive man to consult, but he does – always ... We were in the jewellery department when I noticed that he had become distracted. He is always most attentive when choosing such gifts, and so it was strange to see him staring at a group of people who had just entered the store.

They were strangely dressed, and they looked uncomfortable in their clothes. One man wore a pinstriped suit but had a pair of riding boots on his feet. Another had an open-necked shirt and a waistcoat. Another wore a top hat but was dressed in a lounge suit. One of the females was beautifully dressed as though ready for church on a Sunday morning but she had no hat ... Do you remember the New Look that came in after the war? Well another woman was dressed in what could have been a Dior creation, but she had brogues on her feet. It was very, very weird.

Robert seemed to understand what they were saying, but I couldn't hear a single word. There was an ominous silence, but no distinct speech. Does that make sense? One of these ...

people approached Robert and some conversation seemed to pass between them, although he denied this afterwards when we spoke of the matter. Later, it was almost as though the incident had not occurred – but it wasn't to be an isolated one. Do you know London at all, Emma?"

"No."

"We had emerged from the underground station at South Kensington. Although I would have preferred a taxi, Robert is very fond of the underground and we had just passed through the ticket barrier when we saw this man standing by the public telephone boxes. He seemed undecided as to whether he should use them. Again, he was strangely dressed: sun glasses, a dark grey suit much too big for him and leather boots. He made eye contact with us and asked the way to the Science Museum. I say 'asked' because nothing else makes sense, but I didn't see his mouth move. What do you make of that? His request simply appeared in my mind.

I found myself picturing the route, but I said nothing and neither did Robert. However, no sooner had the picture become clear in my mind than the ... man scurried off in the right direction. I was so fascinated – annoyed, more accurately – that I wanted to follow and see what he was about, but Robert forbad me, and we went on our way."

"Did you talk about the incident afterwards?" asked Emma.

"Robert shrugged it off. You know what men are like when they don't wish to engage in any discussion."

"And you believe these people are connected in some way with your children's disappearance and your husband's ... disturbance?"

"I really don't know, but Robert knew who they were – I'm sure of that fact – and he doesn't seem as perturbed as he might be about the disappearance of Patricia and Myles. It's almost as though he knows they will return ... Oh God, I hope so – and safely."

Emma told me that she stayed until late evening talking over much the same ground time and time again. When she did return and imparted her news to her menfolk, Ernest scratched his head, while George looked puzzled and only Roach spoke.

"The gentleman from Chillesford," he said, "We met him in the Oyster on my first night here."

"What about him, boy?"

"His clothes struck me as odd."

"It'd be very odd if Sir Robert Hargreaves or any other man for that matter was involved in the disappearance of his own children," said Ernest.

"That is what torments Lady Hargreaves," replied Emma.

After the others had gone to bed, Roach lingered for a while in the kitchen before lighting his pipe and leaving the cottage. He was disturbed by what he called in his diary *the extraordinary disconnection of events.* He made his way along Mill Road towards the Oyster and stood on the corner where the Woodbridge to Orford and Campsey Ash to Hollesley roads crossed on their journeys. The night was warm and peaceful, and tomorrow the village would go about its business as usual. As he watched and listened, Roach could hear and see the various cottages and houses closing down for the night: the landlord was rolling an empty barrel into the yard at the back of the pub; lights were being extinguished downstairs; curtains were being drawn before bedroom lights were lit upstairs; doors opened as cats were put out for the night; Jack Stevens passed on his bike; Roach pictured John Bird making a final check on his livestock; in the distance beyond the dark of Rendlesham Forest he heard the sound of a tractor; a courting couple kissed goodnight on Church Road before the girl drifted away into one of the cottages and the boy turned off home across the fields; somewhere a dog barked and rattled its chain; garden sheds were closed as tools were locked up. It was all so normal, as the villagers retired from one day and prepared for the next.

Yet, had Roach taken a pair of compasses and drawn a circle on a map with a radius of no more than a mile and a half from where he stood, more or less every strange event would have been enclosed within the circle: the disappearance of the children, the crash landing of a strange craft, the marks on Wantisden Corner, Norman Bird's visitors, Harry Cole's creatures, the crater between the potato and barley fields, whatever it was that had terrified John Bird's cattle, the strange craft that glowed green and the figures moving in its light seen by PC Heath and his colleague, the experience of John Bird and his farmworker and Steve Lomax's aircraft hovering over the clearing with its beam of bright light and the men in space helmets.

Only the encounters of Geraldine Hargreaves and her husband had occurred many miles away, and their connection with the village seemed to rest in Sir Robert himself.

And yet it was all so disconnected unless you could convince yourself of the ridiculous, Roach wrote. He couldn't have known as he stood on the Oyster corner lighting his third pipe of the evening that the apparent insanity of events would all too soon become abundantly understandable.

CHAPTER 9

Strange Lights in the Sky

Roach's rude awakening – *his arousal from his rural doze*, as he wrote – came with the arrival in the village of Sally Tigg. She did what no normal and decent woman would have done in those days: she walked into the public bar of The Oyster. Sally Tigg was what future generations would call a ufologist; only the term UFO had not been coined in 1955. Back then she was simply an eccentric: mad but harmless.

It was as Ernest Roach's fortnight was nearing its end and he was enjoying a pint with his son and nephew that Sally Tigg walked into the pub, placed her handbag on the bar and ordered a bottle of Guinness. The landlord was taken aback and the locals were stunned into silence. Even Ernest raised his eyebrows and gave his son a warning look.

She was dressed in a pair of heavy, corduroy trousers and a very large overcoat belted round the waist. She'd removed her hat before entering the pub and so her hair hung or flopped all over the place. Her face was so plain that an unkind person might have described Sally Tigg as ugly but for two things: her eyes that shone like bright, black buttons and her hair that, although tousled from being confined beneath her headwear, was an auburn mane.

"Would you be so kind as to point me in the direction of Dot Harris?" enquired Sally, as she poured the beer down her throat, placed the glass back on the bar and ordered a second bottle.

"She lives down the road at Hollesley. About five miles on," replied the landlord.

It suddenly occurred to George to wonder how the lady came to be in Butley at that time of the evening. Nathan Catchpole's coach had passed through on its outward journey some time before.

"It's quite a walk," he said, "Would you care to borrow my bike?"

"How very kind of you, young man, but I am obliged to decline your offer. Thank you, but I have my own transport."

"Where are you from, Mrs ...," began the landlord.

"Miss – Miss Sally Tigg, and I hail from a little town in Surrey called Wallington."

"You've come all the way from Surrey today, have you?"

Sally Tigg smiled at the unbelieving faces staring at her. Several mouths were open in amazement, and even those who looked studiously in any direction but Sally's sat motionless, their hands poised on domino, dart or tankard.

"Yes – all the way."

She was obviously thirsty because she downed the second beer as readily as the first and drew on the gloves she had placed beside her handbag on the bar. It was the movement that drew Roach's attention to the gloves, which he had failed to notice when the woman entered the bar. They were huge, leather gauntlets: the sort worn by motorcyclists. At the same moment, he saw that her headwear was a leather helmet and goggles of the sort worn by airmen during the war.

"You have a motorbike?" he asked, feeling more stupid than the rest of the pub looked.

"I have, young man, and a side car. Thirty pounds it cost me, including the sidecar. Would you like a ride?"

"One of my friends had a Norton when we were doing trade training at RAF Compton Bassett. We'd go into Calne on our days off. It was great fun," replied Roach, with that amiable grin he used so well.

"Are you the young man from the RAF?"

"I was, but I'm ..."

"We need to talk. Dot told me about you. You were in the forest the night the saucer landed, weren't you?"

"Whoa, just a minute," said Roach, quietly, "Who's Dot and who told her I was in any forest on any night?" asked Roach.

"Don't be reticent, Mr Roach. You've been poking your nose into the mystery, and I like people who poke their noses into mysteries. I'm a professional nose poker. Sally Tigg! How do you do."

"How do you do," answered Roach, shaking the proffered hand from which the gauntlet had been removed.

"Look, I've no time to waste tonight, Mr Roach. Dot will be expecting me and she'll be worried if it gets dark before I arrive. What time do you open in the morning," she asked the landlord, over her shoulder, and before he could answer, replied to her own question, "Noon, I suppose. When will we catch up with the continent? I'll be here at 12 o'clock tomorrow morning, and we'll have a chat. I'm sure you've lots to tell me, and I certainly have a mine of information for you."

With that comment, Sally waved a jolly cheerio to the locals and walked out through the door. Fascinated, Roach followed her and watched as she mounted and kick-started her motorbike. It was a BSA Bantam. Just briefly, he envied this middle-aged woman. While the rest of the country made do with push bikes and dreamed of the cars they saw in American films, Sally Tigg had joined the progressive thinkers of the day and bought a motorbike. Roach watched her whizz off down the road to Hollesley.

The following day, she was as good as her word and brought the Bantam to a shuddering halt outside The Oyster at noon precisely. The day was as hot as many another had been that summer, and so Sally's motorcycle gear was abandoned for a tweed two-piece suit. She wore no hat and her hair flowed back in the wind of her ride until the length of it settled in a magnificent heap on her shoulders.

Roach was sitting on a bench outside the pub with a pint already half drunk. Sally shook his hand and ordered him another, and a double gin and tonic for herself, by belting the order through an open window before Roach had time to make the polite offer.

"Now, Mr Roach – what is your name, by the way?"

"Dave."

"May I call you Dave?"

"By all means," Roach replied and, apart from Emma, she was the only person who ever did use his Christian name. By tradition, even at school, we all used each other's surnames with the greatest familiarity. I think that only my parents ever called me James.

"Now, Dave, Tell me all you know, and then I'll place your information against a background that will make your jaw drop off – a panorama of disbelief."

Using his diary, Roach ran over in detail every incident to which he had become privy, and Sally Tigg listened without interrupting him once.

"And so what do you make of all these strange happenings, Dave? Happenstance, coincidence or ... What would we have called it during the war – enemy action?"

"I don't know what to make of it."

"Oh yes you do! You just won't let yourself admit it."

Her bright, black eyes bored into his head, while her mouth smiled knowingly.

"Now, allow me to answer the questions you raised last night and then paint for you my panorama of disbelief. My friend, Dot Harris, who is a psychic investigator ..."

"A what?" Roach asked.

"A psychic investigator! She investigates paranormal activity. You will have heard of the Society for Psychical Research?"

"No."

"They investigate hauntings, ghosts, out-of-body experiences – you seem stunned, Dave?"

"Are you suggesting that these creatures I have described are ghosts?"

"No, no, no – far from it. But we are not going to get very far if you keep interrupting me. Dot is much too busy investigating a haunted rectory, and so she passed this information on to me."

"I do apologise, Miss Tigg. Please go on," urged Roach.

"Sally – my friends call me Sally. Now may I continue? Dot Harris was contacted by an American friend who works on the base – in fact he works on both bases, Bentwaters and Woodbridge. They are, you know, really one American Air Force Unit separated only by the forest. It was he who mentioned your expedition into the forest, and how Lieutenant Colonel Humphreys waylaid you. He – Dot's friend, that is – was one of the first on the scene. When he and his colleagues reached the clearing in question they came upon what can only be described as a flying saucer. The craft was circular in shape with a dome on top and a series of glowing lights ..."

"They actually saw this craft for themselves?"

"Please, Dave ..."

"I'm sorry. I won't interrupt again."

"Rendlesham Forest is private land owned by the British Forest Commission. When Dot's contact came across this craft he immediately contacted the British police who sent two officers into the forest ..."

"And was it these officers ... Sorry."

"Dot's contact was absolutely certain that this was a spaceship from another world."

"What did ...? Sorry."

"They couldn't get close enough to see properly. The saucer was surrounded by this blinding, white light but they were sure the craft was supported on three legs. Our boys in blue must then have contacted the base because it was at this stage in the proceedings Lieutenant Colonel Pat Humphreys, who is Deputy Base Commander, became involved. He organised a team to investigate and, of course, Dot's contact accompanied the team into the forest, since he had been one of the first on the scene. What they found in the clearing was, indeed, amazing. Several small creatures appeared to be working on their spaceship as though it had been damaged in the crash. Lieutenant Colonel Humphreys immediately had the area cordoned off – hence, your road blocks, Dave – and before long the area was swarming with American service personnel. Dot's contact remained on the scene, although at a distance from the main activity, and he swears that the whole incident was filmed by the Americans ... But the most interesting piece of information of all is that one of the space creatures must have been killed because Dot's contact swears that a coffin was brought into the clearing and a body removed. What do you think of that?"

"May I interrupt?"

"Of course."

"Two questions: what did these creatures look like, and how is such an incident to be kept secret if so many people are in the know?"

"As far as secrecy is concerned, I imagine there will be severe de-briefings, threats against witnesses who might be tempted to talk to the newspapers and that many of the servicemen concerned will be dispersed to other bases across the world. This is the usual practice in these matters. As for your second question: he didn't get a close look at the creatures working on the craft, but said that they looked like traditional spacemen – the type we are familiar with through comics and films."

"Doesn't that strike you as significant, Sally?"

"In what way?" she asked, *her voice flecked with asperity*, Roach wrote in his diary.

"Never mind ... Why should all this be happening around here in this quiet, Suffolk backwater – or is that a stupid question?"

"It's a stupid question because you know the answer as well as I do," Sally replied, "Apart from the two NATO air bases, which would be of extreme interest to intelligent beings from outer space, we have the secret laboratories at Orford Ness, an experimental electronics station at Martlesham, the RAF site at Bawdsey where rumours abound about interesting experimental work, radar stations situated at Watton, Lakenheath and Neatishead, and then there is Shingle Street where the entire village was evacuated during the war. This 'quiet, Suffolk backwater' of yours, Dave, is a hive of top secret activity; and where better to conduct such activity than in a remote area devoid of public transport?" said Sally, without a single pause for breath.

"Yes, OK, I admit I can see the reasons why secrecy is paramount. If such a story was leaked we would have mass public panic. So why are you here? What do you want me to do?"

"Just like a man: turn a blind eye when the way forward looks difficult."

"Not at all."

"Yes – at all! We are going to see Lieutenant Humphreys and put a few questions to him."

"Just like that?" exclaimed Roach, quite flabbergasted by the energy and confidence of this redoubtable woman.

"Dot has already been in touch, and he is expecting us."

Lieutenant Colonel Pat Humphreys was *a model of American urbanity* when he greeted them in his office on the base at RAF Bentwaters, and he had invited the RAF base commander, Squadron Leader Douglas Fern, to be present.

"As an additional source of reassurance, Miss Tigg," he said, taking Sally by the hand and leading her to a seat in his spacious office.

She and Roach were disarmed immediately; there could be nothing sinister about a man who exuded so much natural charm, thought Roach. Coffee and 'cookies' – a new word for Roach's vocabulary at the time – were offered and accepted, and they spent the best part of an hour exchanging pleasantries, but little information. Only once did the conversation take an uneasy turn and that was when Sally mentioned RAF Watton.

"I came here at Dot's request," she said, "but I already understood from a friend of mine that there was some concern regarding the tracking of an unknown object across the sky on the night by the staff of RAF Watton."

"We have no military personnel at RAF Watton, Sally," replied Pat Humphreys with great familiarity, "and so I am afraid I can be of little help. Douglas?"

"I have no idea who your contact was, Miss Tigg," said Squadron Leader Fern, "but I imagine it was just pub talk, was it not?"

"I was given to understand that RAF Watton tracked an unknown object across the East Anglian coast north of Great Yarmouth. Whatever this object was, it disappeared off their radar screens in the vicinity of this base."

Pat Humphreys and Douglas Fern looked at each other and wrinkled their eyebrows and smiles in an identical manner. *It was at that moment*, wrote Roach, *that I felt something was amiss.* His feeling was confirmed a few seconds later when Sally waded in with a rather clinching comment.

"Is it not true that intelligence officers from Bentwaters visited RAF Watton and that radar recordings were removed?"

The 'friendly chat' – Pat Humphreys' description of their meeting when Sally and Roach arrived – came to an abrupt end. It seemed that neither Humphreys nor Fern were prepared to be entangled in what they might suppose would soon become a web of lies. Aware that she had obtained information by negation, Sally Tigg persisted no further, and they left amicably.

"American intelligence officers would not have removed radar recordings from an RAF base without permission and unless they could have justified doing so," insisted Sally, as she mounted her BSA Bantam and Roach manoeuvred himself into the sidecar, "To justify such a course of action, they would have had to confide in the British authorities, and that means they would have shared their knowledge of the incident in Rendlesham Forest with some high-ups in the British military."

Roach looked at his watch. It was after two o'clock and The Oyster would now be closed until seven that evening. He wasn't a great drinker in those days but, at the moment, Roach felt he could do with a pint.

Had he, now, any doubts that something unusual was going on, such doubts would have been dispelled in the evening when he and George accompanied his father to The Oyster for a farewell pint before Ernest left for home early the next morning.

It had been uncomfortably hot since Roach arrived in Butley, and everyone was hoping for a storm, "something to clear the air a bit" as one of the farmworkers put it. The heat had certainly built up and the sky, as the night darkened, began to fill with the thunder clouds of summer. Looking up from where they sat on the bench the landlord had placed against the outside wall, Roach and his father and cousin were expecting a summer storm: a sudden burst of cooling rain to take the heat out of the air and settle the dust. It might only last minutes but it would be a welcome relief from the heat of the day. When the first sheets of lightning crackled across the sky, several of the regular domino players left their game to watch. The black clouds moved with a suddenness familiar in the countryside and the first drops of heavy rain fell like hailstones. Roach felt the joy of catching them in his hands. His companions pressed themselves back against the wall of the pub but made no attempt to go inside as the rain began to fall more steadily and solidly. On such a night, a man could dry on the way home, watching the vapour rise from his clothes.

It was while they were watching the lightning and drinking in the rain that all of them saw a ball-shaped object emerge from beneath the layer of cloud. Roach recorded that he *felt his spine tingle at the sight*. When a green light began to pulse within the body of the object, he experienced apprehension followed by immediate terror. A whirring sound could be heard beneath the crackles of lightning and the object shot straight up into the clouds. Roach glanced at his companions; all eyes were fixed on the sky. Whatever it was had travelled in from the east, from across the North Sea in the direction of Orford Ness.

Roach remembers wanting to ignore the sight – not wanting to believe what he had seen – when the object appeared again.

He judged it to be at an angle of twenty degrees to the horizon and travelling westward towards Bentwaters. Tilted as it now was, the object resembled one of those sweets he had enjoyed as a child – the sort with a flattened outer rim and a central ball filled with sherbet – rather than a sphere. Roach remembers laughing at the thought and the looks of reprimand he received from the locals. The object was metallic and now shone with a bluish light. It skirted the treeline surrounding the base and then rose vertically and rapidly into the air before disappearing once more into the clouds.

They all waited for many minutes but saw no more of the strange object. After a while, one of the domino players looked round at the others, his face a picture of unnatural fear.

"I've never seen anything like that before," he said, "Ball lightning, I suppose. You get that with a summer storm. I've seen it red and yellow and sometimes white, but I ain't seen it green or blue 'til now."

"No," said one of the other players, "and I ent seen it last for more than a few seconds at a time before either."

"Anyone fancy another pint?" asked Roach, catching his father's eye and suddenly realising it had stopped raining. Afterwards, he noted that all he wanted to do at that moment was not talk about what they had seen because *talking would have acknowledged a truth he could scarcely bear to believe.*

They re-entered the pub to enjoy a final beer and to dry off from the sudden cloudburst. As they sat quietly wondering but not wishing to share their thoughts, the locals were unaware their sighting of this unidentified object had been experienced by a courting couple who had been spending some time in the forest. Forty years later, the couple – now married and with four children – talked of that night to me.

"We were ... you know ... when we heard this whirring sound. The thing was coming in over the cowshed in the next field. It was glowing with this green light and was really low in the sky. It seemed to be moving towards us, and my girlfriend – my wife, now – screamed, and I told her to keep quiet. We didn't want to attract any attention. You could see it was under control. You know how a boat is in the water – you have to allow for the wind and the current and give just enough engine power to overcome them but no more? It was like that. Whoever was steering it knew what they were doing. The thing was there was no noise apart from that faint whirring sound. Not like you get with a normal plane. It reached the line of trees and then shot upwards at a helluver burst of speed.

We thought that was it, but no. We rushed over to the wire fence that divides the forest from the field. We wanted to get way from there as fast as we could, I can tell you. From there you can see over towards the base – not the actual runways but the belt of trees that surround it – and we could see it coming in to land. It was coming straight down and there were lights, really bright they were, all round the rim: orange, yellow – it was hard to tell in the dark."

Sally Tigg, some six or seven miles further down the Suffolk coast at Hollesley had seen and heard nothing. As Roach and his family downed their final pints and the courting couple ran from Rendlesham Forest, she was easing back the little lever on her fountain pen to refill it from the bottle of Quink ink. Dot Harris had gone to bed early, leaving Sally the time she needed to complete her article for the *Flying Saucer Review*, a UK magazine that saw its first light of day that year.

CHAPTER 10

The Gent from Chillesford

As Roach waved his father goodbye on Nathan Catchpole's coach the next morning, he was glad to see him go. His father belonged to the real world and not this nightmare from outer space. Before he could venture into this strange new universe, Roach wanted his father out of the way, at home and safe. Roach admitted in his diary that up until the moment he saw the spaceship there had been doubts; up until that moment, he held the role of the sceptic. Despite Sally Tigg's assertions, or perhaps because of them, he felt there must be a more earth-bound explanation for the events about which he had been told. But now, he had no reservations at all in linking the appearance of the space ship with the disappearance of the children, with the creatures that had bedevilled the quietude of John Bird and his family and the other sightings the likes of Steve Lomax preferred to forget.

His mind was made up. Terror had stalked his sleep since the appearance of the strange spacecraft, and it was time to do something about it. He should have gone to the forest last night but he had been too stunned to think clearly: too stunned and afraid. He knew that now. He had to acknowledge his fear. His father's safety hadn't been Roach's only concern the previous night; he had been scared. Scared of finding the craft and scared of what it would most certainly hold – denizens of another world. The phrase had been a joke but not anymore.

He estimated that Bentwaters airbase (like the Woodbridge one, where the first craft had crash landed) must be over two miles long: the landing strip alone would make such a demand. It was a question of where to head. The craft had disappeared beyond the trees west of Wantisden Common. Jack Stevens would loan him a bike – he might even come with him – but should he use the track across the common or should he take the longer route? This would mean using the minor road to Friday Street, which was situated near the end of the runway: a more discreet place, perhaps, for a spaceship to land.

It will no longer be there, of course. Anyway, how am I to gain access to the base, which is surrounded by high fences and must be crawling with security patrols? Indeed, what am I intending to do? What is the point of going into the forest at all? Will there be anything to find when I arrive?

The turmoil in Roach's mind was evident in the night's diary entry. He had not slept. Visions of despair had crossed his mind. Overnight his natural self-confidence seemed to drain away. The discord had been building up, of course, ever since he heard of the disappearance of the children. *How had Tom Ward described it? Like the extraction of a bad tooth? A vacuum in the air: the empty feeling when there's nothing there, just the hole.* And there had been that strange business of the visitors in Norman Bird's bedroom. *"... they came over to the bed and looked at me ... They didn't seem to want to play then ..."* What had they wanted? *"To have those creatures touching you – their ... hands ... can you call them hands? ... doing things to you."* John Bird's experience on the river bank came to Roach's mind followed by the words of Steve Lomax. *"Three creatures were standing round me. At first I thought they were insects, but when I yelled they seemed more human."* Jumping and twisting around amidst all these disparate thoughts were Myles and Patricia Hargreaves: *still missing, but somewhere – possibly.*

He was unusually quiet when he returned from seeing his father onto the coach. When Emma commented on the fact, Roach explained what was on his mind.

"I'll come with you," offered George.

"No ... but thanks, anyway. I have an uneasy feeling about this business, George. Like everybody else, I've been putting off a decision but I've made up my mind now. You're a family man – or will be one day," he said, smiling at Emma, "and I have no responsibilities except to myself and my conscience. If those lights were part of what people call a flying saucer, whoever was in the craft had a purpose in coming here. It's twice that this spot has been visited in less than a month. The first time it happened was around the time the Hargreaves children disappeared."

"Just after," suggested George.

"As far as we know but we just don't know much about these craft, do we? Was it hanging about up there beyond our vision? Where are the children?"

"What are you going to be looking for, Dave?" asked Emma.

"I'm hoping to find evidence that a space craft landed in the forest or on the base last night."

"In that case, perhaps this will be of use to you," replied Emma, who took a Kodak Box Brownie camera from one of the kitchen drawers. "It was my mother's. It's got flash and a close-up lens. It'll work in the forest."

"Thanks, Emma. I'll bring it back safely."

"Please just bring yourself back safely ... Do you really think you'll be able to get on to the base?"

"Harry Cole mentioned that rabbits were plentiful on the base, and I think he might know of a way, but we'll see."

Emma told me all those years later that Roach was agitated throughout the whole of the morning's conversation; so restless both in his manner and his movements that she watched anxiously as he left for the poacher's cottage.

Harry Cole's terrier, Reggie, welcomed Roach at the gate and Harry Cole ushered him into the front room.

"Would you like a cup of tea, Mr Roach? Reggie's all right now, thanks to you."

The room was unexpectedly neat and tidy for a man's home, thought Roach, as he sipped from the mug of tea. It was a dull morning, since the clouds of the previous night still hung in the air, but the subdued light, easing gently in through the lattice windows, suited the quiet of the time and the peacefulness of the room. Roach promised himself he'd get a dog when he eventually found a place to live.

Harry Cole listened attentively while Roach explained his intentions. Years later, he told me that he "hadn't slept since that night" and had difficulty "catching his breath". Roach seemed calm, he said, and determined, but Harry couldn't face the idea of venturing close to the base so soon after another landing. He suggested Roach should make his way towards the Friday Street end of the base where the fence could be eased off the ground near where a great beech stood, "the one that's been struck by lightning", and that – approaching through the forest – Roach might stand a chance of reaching the base unnoticed. He felt ashamed at his cowardice but "couldn't face another scare so soon – another saucer having landed the previous night". Roach understood and was leaving when Harry called him back.

"I dursn't come, Mr Roach, but you take this with you – just in case", he said, and handed Roach his twelve-bore.

"I can't think what use I'll have for a shotgun, Mr Cole."

"Take it. If you see any of the creatures I saw, you'll need it," replied Harry.

It was obviously a treasured possession, and Roach respected the offer. He slipped a supply of cartridges into his pocket, and nestled the gun under his arm in the broken position.

"Follow the stream across the north of the park and you'll pick up the trail off the common. Keep to that until you come within half-a-mile of Friday Street and then cut along north to the edge of the airfield," Harry called out as Roach made off.

It was a pleasant enough walk even on that dull morning – today it is part of the Suffolk Sandlings Walk from Sutton Common to Butley – and Roach's feelings of guilt soon left him to be replaced by a sense of purpose. He enjoyed the sight of the willow stems rising out of the stream and watched caterpillars feeding on the leaves of the tree. A sedge warbler darted in and out of the yellow irises, picking at all it could find, its sharp eyes seeking insects that in their turn were determined to stay alive by adopting as camouflage the appearance of their backgrounds. Floating on the water was what he thought were the leaves of watercress. Here, the stream flowed gently with only a soft rippling sound above which could be heard the songs of several birds.

In the fields beyond, Roach saw rows of neatly hoed sugar beet and the pale green shoots of young oats. Further still, was the golden stubble of the harvest fields. Above the common, a meadow pipit trilled its song; he watched the bird rise in flight and glide earthwards with a final trill. His grandfather had walked him as a child and talked to Roach about the birds, and he remembered being distressed when told that the cuckoo used the little pipit to rear its own fledglings.

Soon the open walk became enclosed on both sides by the forest; first, a mix of conifers and beeches and silver birches, and then dominated by the dark and brooding pines. Beyond these to Roach's right was RAF Bentwaters, but it was as invisible to him as it was absent from any current maps. Even so, Roach could not believe it was "a hive of top secret activity" as Sally Tigg had claimed – or, if it was, the activity had nothing to do with visitors from outer space. His nature walk began to dispel his doubts; after all, what could be amiss in such beautiful countryside?

He found the beech described by Harry Cole quite easily. A tree blasted by lightning is a sorry sight, and yet it provided a home for beetle grubs and a source of food for the green woodpecker, which had pecked several large holes in the trunk. Two young jays were perched in its branches and threatened by a grey squirrel that approached them along the top rail of a fence. An adult jay, knowing the threat posed by the squirrel, was scolding it. Roach's grandfather had a strong dislike of grey squirrels, knowing them to have been introduced from America and to have driven out our native reds and to be a menace both to birds and their eggs. He looked at the marauder with its long, sharp teeth and wondered whether or not to pitch a stick at it, but the squirrel saw him first and disappeared rapidly.

Around the base of the tree, young bracken fronds were unfolding; these formed a strong line from the tree to the fence of the airfield. Roach crouched down among them and began to examine the fence itself. It was while he was stooped in this manner that he became aware of the old man. He was still dressed in the purple waistcoat, the corduroy trousers, the knee-length boots, the hat that was a cross between a trilby and a top hat and the long yellow coat with the velvet collar that had struck Roach as out of place when they had met that first night in The Oyster. He still spoke in the old, soft voice: a voice that soothed and controlled.

"Mother Nature is wonderful," he said, "Always she finds a way, a use for even the dying tree. Where would we be without her?"

The tone of the speech had a certain mocking quality, noted Roach, as though the man didn't quite mean what he said or, perhaps, didn't believe it at all.

"She always finds her way," the gent from Chillesford continued, "even if sometimes she benefits from a little nudge."

Roach rose to his feet and extended his hand, which the gent from Chillesford declined.

"I'm Dave Roach," he said, "We met in The Oyster."

"Erasmus Darwin," said the gent from Chillesford in reply, and the answer seemed to amuse him, "Are you interested in nature, Mr Roach?"

"In passing, but not professionally. I've just completed my National Service. I was a wireless operator in the RAF."

"Hence your interest in flying machines?"

Erasmus Darwin – *was that really his name*, wrote Roach that evening – had a good memory: aircraft was the subject of Roach's conversation with Harry Cole on that first evening.

"You have some medical knowledge, I seem to remember," asked Roach.

"I have extensive medical knowledge, Mr Roach ... far beyond anything you might imagine. I am what your countrymen once called a natural philosopher and a physician. You have heard of my namesake – Erasmus Darwin?"

"No, I can't say I have."

"He was the grandfather of the famous Charles. You will have heard of him?"

"Yes," replied Roach, wondering where the conversation was leading, "One of our teachers was an admirer."

"Quite rightly so! Your Mr Darwin very cleverly hit upon the secret of the survival of any species."

"The survival of the fittest?"

"That is a very crude way of expressing a very subtle theory of evolution, if you will excuse my saying so, Mr Roach. The secret of survival for any species is its capacity to adapt to a changing environment. Failure to do so results in extinction; whole worlds have thus died. Mr Darwin pointed out – and, indeed, established – that this capacity is determined by natural selection – a process of which the animal itself will be unaware.

Much of his early research was stimulated, however, not by observing natural selection but by observing what one might call unnatural selection – breeding for a specific purpose. He was fascinated by the way pigeon fanciers bred winners by selecting the best flyers and obliging them to mate."

The gent from Chillesford smiled as he spoke, as though the idea of obliging pigeons to mate amused him. Did he smile or was it the tone of voice? Roach wasn't sure.

"And, of course, the very wide varieties of dogs we see about the villages were all created by unnatural selection. Every single one of them selectively bred from the grey wolf, which resembles few of them in appearance but whose genetic code is identical."

"I'm sorry," apologised Roach, "genetic code?"

"Ah, words yet to be understood by most of your species, Mr Roach. An idea yet to be assimilated into your language," replied the gent from Chillesford, laughing.

There was a long pause while he looked me up and down, wrote Roach, *and this was followed by an almost grandfatherly smile.* The old man walked away from Roach a few paces and then turned as though considering whether or not to continue the conversation. Afterwards, Roach wondered why he was a subject of interest at all to this 'natural philosopher'. *Perhaps it was just a human need to share an understanding.*

"You are clearly an intelligent young man, Mr Roach, but I imagine that the level of your scientific knowledge is lamentably low. Would I be correct?"

"I wouldn't put it as strongly as that," Roach replied, "but my interests lie more in the area of physics than in biology."

"We talked of the great variety of dogs. However different in appearance and despite the many varieties they are the same species. But let us consider equus caballus and equus asinus," the gent continued with a broad smile, "They are closely related but they are two distinct species – the horse and the donkey. Yet they have been successfully bred to produce a mule. Might one call this unnatural production, this third species, equus mulus?"

Anyone warming to their subject was always a great joy to Roach. When I thought I was boring him in Sharjah as I explained the workings of the desalinisation unit, I glanced at his face for reassurance and reassurance was written all over it. It was the same now as he listened to the gent from Chillesford who had called himself Erasmus Darwin.

"I know what you're thinking, Mr Roach: a species cannot be considered a species unless it is capable of producing offspring and mules are always infertile. Am I right?"

"I wish you were. My knowledge doesn't extend to the fertility of mules," answered Roach, no doubt in that disarming way of his, "but you are still ahead of me ...You are telling me that mules have produced offspring and that a third species has been produced from a previous two?"

"Exactly!"

Roach was still unsure where the conversation was leading. This many years on it may seem clearer (and may make him seem unfairly dense) because our use of scientific terminology – whether or not we always understand what we are talking about – is more widespread, but in 1955 genetics was not under discussion in the public domain.

"Do I make you wonder?" asked the gent from Chillesford.

"Just a trifle," said Roach, and at that moment he began to understand – not the science of the old man but the purpose. *I was petrified,* he wrote in his diary, *I was frightened that he was taking me into his confidence, and sensed not only danger but death. I was haunted by the words 'unnatural selection'.*

"There's no need to be afraid, Mr Roach. I mean you no harm. I rarely have the chance to share my enthusiasm with one of your species, and this talk in the forest is a joy to me. Although you do not have the words to understand, you do have the intelligence to appreciate what I am telling you."

"Go on," said Roach, fingering the cartridges in his pocket.

"To produce a mule a female horse may be bred with a male donkey, or a male horse with a female donkey. In the first case, the resultant mule will be male; in the latter it will be female. Sometimes, your people call this female mule a hinny. Yes?"

"I believe so."

"Whether male or female, the mule possesses the best qualities of both horse and donkey – qualities it will pass on to its offspring. Yes?"

"Yes."

"The mule is more patient, sure-footed, hardy and longer-lived than the horse; and is less obstinate, faster and more intelligent than the donkey. Am I right?"

"Go on."

"Suppose that your species could be thus improved – and yet not by sexual reproduction, which would not be possible. Would this not be a good thing?"

Roach was thinking that *the world had just been here,* when the gent from Chillesford captured his thoughts.

"I did say not by sexual reproduction, Mr Roach."

"Then how?"

"Ah – you are interested! Good!"

"Within each species there is what we might call the thread of life. You must accept that idea, Mr Roach, for you do not have the words for me to be more specific. This thread of life exists in all animals – from the humblest amoeba to your own, complex species. This thread of life endows your species with all the characteristics that make you human.

Now, cast your mind back to your schooldays and to what must have been, as a physicist, one of your favourite subjects – mathematics. Did you not enjoy constructing mathematical models with your milk straws: pyramids, cubes, dodecahedrons? Imagine an infinite number of pyramids, each constructed from three equilateral triangles, linked together in an endless chain. Think of this as your thread of life, and suppose our endless chain to have been constructed of white milk straws.

Now, the dog also has its thread of life. Imagine this to have been created using, say, blue milk straws. The dog's thread of life also endows it with all the characteristics that make it canine.

If we were able to remove any number of your white milk straws from any number of the pyramids that constitute your thread of life, and replace them with the blue milk straws that constitute a dog's thread of life what do you suppose would happen?"

"Human beings would take on some of the characteristics of dogs?"

"Exactly! And we would have produced a separate species, would we not? This new species would have many of the characteristics of both parent species, but it would be quite distinct."

"And this new species would be perpetuated in any offspring?"

"Yes."

"This thread of life – where is it situated?"

"Within each of the billions of cells that make up the animal's body, all of which stem from the one cell – the fertilised egg of the female of the species."

And now Roach knew, as nearly as he could at that time, what was happening. *Without being able to express any of my thoughts in words*, he wrote, *I somehow knew the implications of what he was telling me for my species. I knew, quite instantly, where the Hargreaves children fitted into this picture of the world he was painting and, more or less, what had happened with the Birds and Steve Lomax. I knew that this old man was not human, but a different species from another world.*

"You may know that all the egg cells each female is capable of producing in her lifetime are there in the ovaries at birth."

"Is this what has been happening with the Hargreaves children?"

"We have made certain adaptations."

"But you can't do this to every female on the planet!"

"We do not have to, Mr Roach. We need only adapt those who will lead."

"I don't understand. I can't take this in. Who the hell are you?"

The words of Sir Robert came back to Roach as he struggled to understand: 'We need leaders who possess the wisdom to embrace change, and thus ensure the survival of ... our species.' But what species? What the hell had Sir Robert and his children got to do with this creature that was standing before Roach at this moment?

"Who are you?" he repeated.

"Our planet died long ago, Mr Roach, and those of us who were selected to survive came to your Earth in the hope that we might find a home here ..."

"How long ago?"

"One thing at a time, Mr Roach."

Roach was now peering intently at the gent from Chillesford and realised for the first time that his mouth was not moving.

"You're not speaking. Your mouth's not moving and yet I'm hearing you ..."

"One thing at a time, Mr Roach."

"Are you what you seem to be – a rather dotty old man fascinated by the fauna and flora of our planet – or are ... do you actually ... Are you one of the creatures Harry Cole saw?""

"Calm down, Mr Roach! We were coming to an understanding."

"The flying saucer that I saw last night – what was it doing here?"

"It brought the children back, didn't it? After you'd done what you wanted to them."

The third voice came from the forest. It was the voice of John Bird, who carried his shotgun unbroken. Both Roach and the gent from Chillesford turned to face the newcomer.

"I bumped into Harry Cole, Mr Roach. He was concerned for your safety but scared of this lot. You ain't what you seem, are you? You don't even look the way you seem, do you? What did you want with my boy – heh? What did you want with me when I was out fishing – heh? Stand aside, Mr Roach."

As he spoke, John Bird walked towards Roach and the gent from Chillesford. Roach, fearful of what the farmer intended to do, took a step towards him to prevent the shot, but he was brushed aside, as John Bird raised the shotgun and fired, not once but twice. The gent from Chillesford received both barrels in what had appeared to be his chest and his whole body exploded before them. The purple waistcoat, the corduroy trousers, the leather boots, the hat and the long yellow coat with the velvet collar disappeared completely, as though they had never existed. On the ground before them they saw the shattered remains of what might have been a giant beetle or cockroach. The head was still attached to the stricken thorax and the abdomen was burst open. The wings lay awry and the three sets of legs along the left-hand side of the body were scattered around the corpse.

Roach wrote, later, that had John Bird not fired the shot he might have done, so angry was he at the creature that now lay dead at their feet. *What might have stopped me,* he wrote, *was the thought that there was so much more to learn.* Years later, when John Bird confessed this killing to me as we sat drinking red tea in his kitchen, he more or less confirmed what Roach had written and said Roach had insisted that he should take responsibility for the shooting should any blame be apportioned.

"You're a family man, Mr Bird, and we don't know how the authorities might react."

Roach told the farmer to return home and look after his family. He then took several photographs of the corpse using Emma's camera and retrieved parts of the wings, legs and shell of the creature that resembled an insect. It might take some time for the nearest branch of Boots in Woodbridge to develop the photographs since they would have to send them away for processing, but once that was done he would take them and the body parts to the authorities. The evidence that creatures from another world were here on our planet was now irrefutable. Whether they would believe Roach's account of what the gent from Chillesford had told him remained to be seen.

CHAPTER 11

Asylum

The authorities were not inclined to believe Roach as he discovered very rapidly. Partly on Emma's advice and partly because of his own impatience, he reported the incident immediately, omitting to mention the photographs – again on Emma's advice – but taking with him the collected remains of the creature's body. He approached Jack Stevens initially and the local bobby contacted the duty desk in Woodbridge. The same day a car arrived for Roach. A car in 1950s' Britain was an unusual sight – in Butley and the surrounding area only Sir Robert and the local doctor possessed a car – and the village children, enjoying their summer holiday, lined the road to Woodbridge as the Hillman Husky drove off with Roach in the back.

At the police station, Roach was eased into a bare room and a constable suggested that he might like to take a seat at the one piece of furniture: a large, rather stark looking table on the other side of which were a row of five chairs. The only other furniture in the room was a grey filing cabinet. Roach noticed that the windows were barred. The paintwork was bottle green up to the dado rail with a pallid magnolia above: the standard colours of rooms in public buildings at that time. The ceiling was white but stained a light yellow by tobacco smoke. He was offered a cup of tea and told that he could smoke. While Roach filled his pipe, the constable who had travelled with him in the back of the Husky remained at the door, having issued Roach's request for the tea to another officer.

Eventually, five men entered the room and looked Roach up and down before speaking. They placed a number of files on the table and the one who appeared to be the leader rested a battered briefcase in front of him on the table. He gestured the others to sit and then spoke to Roach.

"Mr Roach, my colleagues and I represent a small working party attached to the Ministry of Defence. We report our findings to the Directorate of Scientific Intelligence and Joint Technical Intelligence Committee. Our working party comprises two scientists and three intelligence officers from the three armed forces," he said, gesturing towards his colleagues as he spoke.

(This was the body that came to be known – once these secret files were opened to the public in 2008, following the Freedom of Information Act of 2005 – as The Flying Saucer Working Party.)

"We understand that you have information that might be of interest to us. Please narrate your story as you see fit. You will not be interrupted. Should we need to clarify any matter we shall do so from our notes when you have finished."

With a nod he dismissed the police constable who had been standing at the door and made himself as comfortable as the wooden chair permitted. Roach noticed that each of the men had removed a notebook from his file and placed it open on the table. As Roach shuffled his feet, five fountain pens were removed from five jacket pockets and their tops unscrewed.

Roach began to feel both uneasy and a fool. As he told his tale and the faces before him remained immobile, his sense of foolishness increased. He began with the sighting of the strange craft and then moved on to his meeting in Rendlesham Forest. His words seemed no more than ramblings as he tried to outline the gent from Chillesford's 'subtle theory of evolution': unnatural selection, genetic code, a third species produced from a previous two, the thread of life, this new species would have many of the characteristics of both parent species but it would be quite distinct.

Only when he had finished and the sweat was pouring from him did the leader of the working party speak.

"Time, I think, for a cup of tea."

He nodded to one of his colleagues who poked his head out into the corridor. Ten or so minutes later a constable appeared with a tray containing a large brown teapot, six cups and saucers with spoons, a jug of milk, a basin of sugar and a plate of rich tea biscuits. During that time no one had uttered a word. Only when the tea was poured and sips had been taken did the leader open up the interrogation to questions.

"You say that everyone in the ... Oyster saw what you supposed to be a space craft? What were their observations?"

"They thought the lights were caused by ball lightning but, as I explained, ball lightning doesn't behave in the way this craft did. This craft was flying. It approached at a definite angle to the horizon and was under control. It was able to rise vertically at a rapid speed. No known aircraft can make such a manoeuvre. I'm familiar with normal aircraft. I've seen a Hunter attempting to pull out of a dive ..."

"Yes, we have your National Service record, Mr Roach. So what do you suppose this object was?"

"In my view it was not a craft that could have been designed or built on Earth."

All five members of the committee glanced along the table at each other as Roach offered this opinion.

"So where do you suppose it might have come from?"

"I don't know. I have no idea. I'm simply telling you what I saw."

"Well, if it wasn't designed and built here on Earth, presumably it must have come from some other heavenly body – Mars, Venus, Jupiter?"

Roach felt his anger rising at what he believed to be the mocking tone of this man's voice, and the leader of the committee intervened.

"Mr Roach, you say that the ... gent in the forest talked of 'genetic experiments'?"

"I said that he used the phrase 'genetic code', which means nothing to me, and that he talked of 'unnatural selection'. I took this to mean that he was implying interference with ... the way things are done naturally – yes, experiments, if you like to use that phrase."

"And you have reason to suppose that these were linked with the disappearance of Sir Robert Hargreaves' children?"

"He talked of making 'certain adaptations'."

"To Sir Robert's children?"

"That was the implication."

Another glance passed along the line of faces, which was followed by a long silence in which Roach felt obliged to say:

"He talked about his planet dying and the survivors coming to Earth to find a home. This seemed connected with his talk of 'adaptations by unnatural selection'."

"Hmm."

It is surprising how annoying a simple 'hmm' can be especially when a person feels that they are talking nonsense. Roach was now on the edge. He had no wish to believe in flying saucers and creatures from another world himself, let alone try to persuade a group of scientists that the ridiculous was true.

"What prompted you to shoot this man, Mr Roach?"

'One lie begets another', his mother had always told him and his protection of John Bird's action now placed him in an untenable position.

"I suppose it was the thought of what these creatures might be doing," he lied.

"But you shot at what you thought was a human being."

"No, by that time I realised he only appeared to be human but was, in fact, one of the creatures ..."

"One of the creatures ...?"

Roach did not want to mention Harry Cole's experience and left unfinished his sentence. Instead, he reached down for the bag he had brought with him and slid the contents onto the table.

"Once he was shot, the creature exploded and this is all that was left. Rather a large beetle, isn't it gentleman – not a species known here on this Earth."

The imperturbable masks could not be held against such evidence. The two scientists immediately reached out and picked up the body parts, and Roach saw there was no doubt in their minds that the items of carcase were genuine. They held in their hands the remains of a species similar to the insects of our planet, but which could not be an insect as we know the animal. *Even if they disbelieved everything I said,* wrote Roach later, *the scientists could not dispute the evidence they held.*

"What do you make of Mr Roach's finds, gentlemen?" asked their leader, a tall man with scathing eyes and a head of snow white hair.

"We shall need to examine these most carefully. They will need to be preserved."

"You will find more in the forest," said Roach, "These are only samples. I left the head and thorax where they were. If you would like me to take you to the spot, I would be only too pleased to do so."

"It's a shame you didn't have a camera with you, Mr Roach."

"Yes," replied Roach, "Wasn't it?"

His third lie was engendered by distrust of this committee. At the time, Roach felt he could always produce the photographs at a later date should his word be held in doubt again. The leader watched him closely as he answered; he was a man clearly used to commanding other men, and Roach discovered later that he had been a naval officer during the war. He reached into his briefcase and pulled out a map, which Roach recognised as the Ordnance Survey sheet 150.

"I think the committee need impose on your time no further, Mr Roach. If you would indicate on this map where the body parts are to be found we shall organise a search of the area ourselves. In the meantime, let me thank you for your trouble and arrange for a car to take you ... back."

He spoke quietly to the man on his immediate right who had been making copious notes as Roach talked. The man rose carefully and left the room. A few minutes later he returned, smiled bleakly at Roach and exchanged a few words with the leader of the committee who turned to Roach.

"Mr Roach, would you object if we asked you to undergo a brief medical examination," he asked.

"You think I'm mad?"

"Certainly not. Your explanation was most lucid, but if we are to take these accounts seriously we must be sure our witnesses – if I may use that word – are in the best of health. In your case, we do have your service record, but a further check would put our minds at rest."

"You've heard of similar incidents?" asked Roach, thinking of Sally Tigg's claims.

"Ye-es … you are not alone in recounting such events. Naturally, I cannot go into any details, as these matters must be treated with confidence and discretion, but the fact that a working party such as ours has been set up at all will indicate the government takes such accounts seriously. We are charged with compiling a report and the state of mind of our witnesses – I use that word again! – is of paramount importance."

It all seemed very reasonable and Roach agreed, even cracking a joke as he left to accompany the committee member with the bleak smile to a waiting car.

"You think I may have picked up a bug in Sharjah?" he said, laughing.

"I hardly think so, Mr Roach. The RAF boys are quite punctilious in such matters. I understand, however, that the standard two-year posting has been reduced to one by the Air Ministry in the case of Sharjah because the conditions out there are too severe. Correct me if I'm wrong."

It was quite true and as the car carried him off Roach wondered, briefly, whether the whole incident might have been a delusion brought on by some disease he had acquired in the Middle East. His doubt was only brief. He reached for his bag, which was nestled on his lap, and felt the one piece of evidence he had retained; there was no mistaking the feel of the shell-like substance that had been torn from the shattered carcase of the gent from Chillesford.

His journey was short. The official car turned along the A12 out of Woodbridge and headed towards Ipswich. Roach noticed a large expanse of heathland and then a string of modern bungalows along the roadside. Further on, he noticed a golf course and agreed with Mark Twain that golf was a good walk spoiled. Beyond this he admired the large 1930s houses with their bay windows set back from the road, and then they were turning into the driveway of what appeared to be a very large stately home or perhaps a Victorian hospital. He noticed the green, spear-topped railings and heard the gates close behind the car.

As he eased himself out of the car, Roach looked up and realised that this was, indeed, a purpose-built hospital, so many and uniform were the windows of the building. Two men in white coats were waiting at the front door and he felt his arm taken gently but firmly as he was led across the carpeted foyer with its wood panelling and then along a bare and colourless corridor. There was the jangle of a large bunch of keys, one of which turned in a lock and Roach found himself in a small room furnished only with a divan. The door closed behind him and he thought he heard a sigh of relief.

The truth came to him immediately; he had been incarcerated in what was once called a lunatic asylum but now went under the more friendly title of mental hospital. He wrote, later: *I was instantly aware of two things. Firstly, that the committee either did believe me to be mad or took me very seriously and, secondly, that I must remain very calm. Any show of panic, any exhibition of feelings would label me as hysterical and produce the restraints and needles that would scramble my mind forever.*

He sat on the divan and waited. He heard shouts and bangs, which were at first muffled and then grew louder until the walls reverberated with the sound. There was the clatter of footsteps as someone walked the corridor wearing leather-soled shoes: leather-soled shoes with segs tapped into the heels to stop them wearing down. A face peered at him through the wired security glass of the door. He became aware of the faint tang of urine – a smell that he later discovered always permeated the hospital however thoroughly the patients or staff cleaned up the faecal mess of the previous night. Roach walked over to what he assumed was a window, but discovered that the wooden security shutters were locked. Panic did seize him at that moment, realising that his freedom was in the hands of others.

He returned to the divan and waited. He waited a long time before the door was finally opened and a charge nurse blocked the doorway. During his National Service years, Roach had acquired the knack – not always reliable but useful in his present circumstances – of summing-up another person at first glance. The man in the doorway was clearly ex-forces – the kind of person who enjoyed being made 'senior man' in the billet. The senior man was always in charge whenever the corporal or instructor was absent; the responsibility gave certain types the chance to shove others around. The nurse allowed Roach one flickering smile and said:

"You're the bloke who's been seeing little, green men aren't you?"

Suppressing an urge to say that 'they were more parchment coloured than green', Roach replied in the affirmative, missing the obviously expected 'sir' from his response.

"And flying saucers?"

"You've received a record already?"

"Word gets around. When you're dealing with loonies you don't take any chances. Come with me and we'll see if you can behave yourself at the meal table."

Roach followed the nurse along the corridor and they entered the ward with its parquet flooring, half wood panelled walls, smell of Mansion polish and the inevitable magnolia paint on the upper half of the walls. All the patients stopped to stare at him as he entered: some with a grin, some with a grimace, all assessing him as friend or foe.

The Formica-topped tables had been set out in rows for dinner. Roach was instructed to sit at the nearest end, and later learned that here was where those patients most likely to cause trouble were placed. The more trustworthy patients sat near the serving hatch. One nurse said grace and then the food was passed out through the hatch. Those patients near the hatch began eating their meals in a reasonably dignified manner, while those around Roach shovelled the food into their mouths, all the time glaring at those around them, daring their fellow patients to pilfer what was on their plate. It was a nauseating scene, and Roach felt sick to his stomach. Fortunately, the experience was over in minutes: knives and forks were scattered unused on the table, dropped food was spattered over the floor or the jackets and ties of the inmates.

As soon as the food and tea had disappeared, the patients sat motionless and Roach wondered what they were expecting. He soon found out. Two of the nurses appeared from the backs with two wet towels and started wiping down the patients' jacket lapels, ties and trousers. It was the first time that Roach in his bewilderment had noticed the clothing of his fellow patients. They all wore their own clothes, but what a state they were in! Remembering his mother's anxiety whenever she had to risk putting one of his pullovers into the copper, he assumed that the woollen material must have been boiled because both jackets and trousers were badly shrunk and the shoulder pads in the jackets were out-of-place lumps. The shortened trousers and arms made the patients look ridiculous. *Almost less than human, and more like scarecrows in the field: almost like another species*, he wrote, philosophically. The fact that many of them *wore shoes broken down at the heel, were unable to tie their laces or button their jackets correctly and had had their hair cut in the institutionalized fashion* – the notorious post-war basin cut – only added to the feeling that Roach had found himself domiciled with creatures that were not of this world.

Two incidents then occurred that made Roach wonder whether the gent from Chillesford had not been right and that our species could do with some 'improvement'.

As soon as the wiping down had been completed, another nurse emerged from the office clutching a fistful of cigarettes. The smile on his face made Roach realise that what the man considered to be a game was afoot. He called out a few names and the patients immediately moved towards him, whereupon he tossed the cigarettes into the air. Those whose names had been called grabbed what they could and ran off, hiding the cigarettes in their clothing. The nurse continued calling names but at a faster pace, tossing more cigarettes into the air as he did so. The scramble that ensued may have amused the staff but did nothing for the patients' dignity. An almost riotous fight took place with patients grabbing at the cigarettes as they fell, snatching them from the mouths of others, picking broken shreds from the floor and pushing each other all over the place as they attempted to wrest the treats from those who had gained them.

One patient went completely berserk as he tried to secure a cigarette. The man, agitated beyond belief at his failure to grab one, went for a fellow patient, tearing at his clothes and punching him remorselessly in the face and chest. The charge nurse moved quickly. He grabbed the man and rammed him against the wall. He then crossed his arms and slid them inside the lapels of the man's jacket, before jerking the man forward, turning his wrists in towards the side of his neck and applying pressure. The man's face turned blue and then purple as he lost consciousness and slumped to the floor. The charge nurse stepped back, nodded to a colleague and watched as the patient was dragged away to a secure room.

Roach watched with growing anxiety, realising he had only been in the place a few hours and knowing that he now had a record as a lunatic – a record that would surely discredit anything he might say in the future, assuming he had a future in the world. Rising from the table, it was all he could do to remain calm. He thought of Emma and George and wondered when they would begin to question his absence. When might they expect him to return? Surely, it would be early evening at the latest. Would they begin their enquiries then, and who could they approach? No one knew where he had been taken from the police station in Woodbridge – if it was there he had been questioned.

What Roach couldn't know at the time was that Jack Stevens had kept his ear to the ground – or, more accurately, the police grapevine. When he telephoned from the village post office, his Woodbridge colleagues soon made him aware of what had happened to Roach and Jack lost no time in cycling to Creek Cottage. Nathan Catchpole's midday coach had already passed through Butley on its way to Ipswich, and so George borrowed a bike and he and Jack reached the outskirts of Ipswich, a distance of some fifteen miles, by mid-afternoon. St David's Mental Hospital wasn't a welcoming place and neither were its staff. Jack Stevens did gain admittance to the foyer only to be told that it wasn't visiting day.

"I know it's not visiting day," he replied, politely if curtly, "but we've cycled a long way to get here and the patient was only admitted today."

"The patient is undergoing certain assessments."

"We can wait."

"It may be a long one."

There was nothing professional about the man's demeanour and I later discovered that he was not even qualified as a nurse; the only qualification he did hold was one inaugurated in 1890 which had been a training course for asylum attendants.

"When is visiting day?" asked George.

"Next Tuesday."

"But that's four days away."

"You can count then, china?"

Aware that persisting might worsen Roach's situation, they left, having written him a note which was never delivered.

Far from having any assessment, Roach was actually polishing a dormitory floor when they arrived. This chore was managed by eight patients under the supervision of a staff nurse and involved wielding a device called a bumper that consisted of a heavy wooden base weighed down by an inch thick piece of lead under which resided a brush. As Roach and another seven patients trapesed backwards and forwards with their bumpers, the staff nurse in charge walked up and down the dormitory flicking dollops of a mixture of solvent and Mansion polish onto the floor using a stick. Once Roach had got into the rhythm of bumping, he found the work quite enjoyable; the knack was to gain impetus by swinging the bumper back as far as possible and then swinging it in front of him as he walked. The click, click, click of the bumpers became almost hypnotic and Roach found himself settling into this way of life. After an hour a cloth was applied under the bumpers and the resulting shine was so bright and clear that Roach could see the reflection of his face in the floor. He had spent two years in the forces, including the eight weeks at RAF Bridgnorth where square bashing was the order of the day, and this type of regimentation was second nature to him as it was to the patients at St David's.

CHAPTER 12

Dying Words

Visiting day came none too soon for George and Emma's peace of mind, and in good time for Roach, who had not wasted his four days in the mental hospital. Under increasing stress, he had strapped in his anger and presented his good face to the nurses, rather like a dog begging a treat. Strapping in his anger had not been easy, partly because of his desire to get out and do something about the gent from Chillesford's companions, wherever they might be domiciled, and partly because of the treatment he witnessed meted out to other patients. Roach discovered rapidly that he was on what was called the Refractory Ward. This was dreaded by the nurses when they saw their names listed against it on the duty rosters; it was the ward that housed difficult and obsessive patients.

His first morning started with a supervised walk down the corridor to the toilet block – the backs, as they were called. He could not help but notice the piles of clothes outside the door of each cell and smell the awful stench of stale urine and faeces that permeated the building. Glancing into one room as he passed, Roach noticed a fellow patient sitting on the edge of his bed with the contents of his chamber pot poured over his head. In the middle of his mattress there was a pool of stagnant urine and a mound of excrement. Roach exchanged glances with the nurse who accompanied him and couldn't help feeling sorry for the man: the last thing he would want to do would be to shovel up another's shit at the start of each day.

But then, as they entered the backs, his moment of sympathy changed to one of anger. An old man was standing, his nightshirt tucked up around his backside, dazed and bemused, his frail legs protruding from beneath his shirt, clutching his day clothes in his hands.

"Are you still standing there, you lazy old bastard! Get your fucking clothes on."

When the old man failed to respond, the charge nurse brought his hobnailed boot down hard on the patient's bare foot. The old man screamed in agony and bent forward to clutch at the pain. The nurse grabbed his hair, yanked his head back and landed a punch into the pit of his stomach. The old man screamed again and collapsed on the concrete floor.

"Now, are we getting dressed or do we need another taste of medicine."

The nurse turned and left. Roach helped the old man to his feet and proceeded to dress him. *All right,* wrote Roach later, *the nurse had twenty or more patients to get up, cleaned and dressed; but this old man had no idea where he was let alone what he was supposed to do.*

His four days continued in much the same vein. Even the hour's exercise was an excuse for some staff to take pot shots at the patients with the leather football they kicked around the airing court. For the staff it was a break from the endless, monotonous routine of menial chores, bathing and shaving patients, scrubbing and polishing floors, cleaning windows and making endless cups of tea.

In a sense, his sympathies were with both parties – patient and nurse – but Roach closed off from this unspeakable filth and random violence. His one purpose was to be a good patient and escape. He had heard talk from other patients of how escapes had been made. One man had ripped off a toilet seat, smashed a window and escaped down a drain pipe, while another had used the leather sofa in the day room as a trampoline and vaulted through the window taking the frame and glass with him; both had been recaptured, one with a broken leg. Roach rather favoured the toilet window, but realised that his best chance would be at night and that he would need some form of transport to get away from the area as quickly as possible.

He was at this stage in his thinking when Emma and George arrived on visiting day with Sally Tigg, who had insisted on joining them and tempted both George and Emma by offering a ride on her motorbike: Emma in the sidecar and George on pillion. It had been a breathless journey, especially for George, who had been obliged to hold tight to his trilby lest it blew away in the wind.

Roach was both relieved and terrified by the first information they gave that Myles and Patricia Hargreaves were both home. However awful the situation was inside St David's it was as to nothing compared with what the gent from Chillesford intimated had been done to one or both of those children; and Roach still did not understand exactly what or why. Was some species from another planet conducting experiments on his species in order to produce a third? The very idea was ridiculous, and yet something was up, some foul game was afoot.

As they sat at the table – neatly clothed for visiting day – and talked, the charge nurse floated around, patting heads and muttering reassurances. All the other patients had been dressed in their Sunday best clothes, their hair combed and their ties straightened just before the visitors were admitted, but Roach wore the sports jacket and flannels in which he had arrived, unsullied – as yet – by having been washed at the mental hospital. Emma and George were both relieved at how normal he looked.

"Why do you think they've put you in here?" asked Emma.

"I think ...," began Roach.

"To discredit him," interrupted Sally, "Anything he says now will be put down to the fact that he's a lunatic."

"So you don't think he'll be here forever?"

"I don't think I'll be here tomorrow," replied Roach with a smile, "If you'll help me."

"Are we all happy?" asked the charge nurse, sidling up to the table.

"Has he been a good boy?" replied Sally, "His imagination always did run away with him."

"He's been as good as gold," replied the nurse, patting Roach on the head, "We're thinking of putting him in charge of scrubbing and polishing the dormitory floor. He's a dab had with a bumper."

Despite himself and his experiences with bumpers and polish, Roach could not help smiling. Taking this as Roach's desire to be helpful, the charge nurse patted him on the head once more and moved on to the next table.

"How can we help?" asked Sally.

Roach outlined his scheme with a feeling of relief. It was risky, of course, and if he failed he would be kept under very strict supervision from that moment on, and any further attempts at escaping would be impossible, but escape meant freedom.

"You'll not be able to stay in this area or return to it – at least for a while. I've come across one or two escapees who they've left alone because they posed no threat but if you're caught in the near future you'll go straight to prison," said Sally.

"What do you suggest?" asked Emma.

"I'll explain on the way back. Let's just say that Dave will need all his accoutrements packed in his holdall ready to go. What time do you intend to make the attempt, Dave?"

"It will have to be after lights out, preferably once the staff settles down for the night: say midnight."

"I'll be outside with my motorbike. Turn right outside the gates ... "

"Your hour is almost up," chimed in the charge nurse, approaching their table for the third time and relieving Emma of the basket of goodies she had brought for Roach, "I'll look after these ... Suffolk scones – just like mother used to make." He gave Emma a wink. "And jam and butter – you country people live well. Mr Roach will enjoy these with his afternoon tea when you've gone."

"The nurses are more likely to enjoy them with their afternoon tea," said Roach when the nurse walked off.

"Turn right outside the gates and you'll find me round the corner, parked just up the road."

"Where will you go?" asked Emma, "You can't keep Dave in hiding."

"I'll tell you on the way back," replied Sally, smiling at her little secret. "I've been busy and what I found bears out my researches and suspicions. But rest assured we shall be many miles from here!"

Roach's plan was quite simple. It was the one used by another patient who had escaped from the building only to be caught later because he failed to get far enough away. Anther weak point was the need to fool the staff into believing that one had left the backs and returned to one's room; he had to have himself locked in the toilet at night. However, nothing ventured, nothing gained.

As the patients along his corridor were herded into their rooms that night, Roach was the first to retire. He plumped up his bed – not too much in case he was discovered, but enough to give the immediate impression that he was under the blankets and sheets when the nurse looked in through the wired security window – and then slipped into the toilet block, having left his clothes arranged neatly on the chair in his room. This had distressed him somewhat but his clothes left for the night would give credence to the belief that he was asleep. He only hoped that Sally would be in place and with the clothes he had bought in London on his return from Sharjah. Dressed only in his nightshirt, he waited. His only real chance lay in the nurses not making a thorough check of the toilets, and Roach simply trusted to the fact that they had enough to do otherwise.

His trust was rewarded. All but the emergency night lights were extinguished along the corridor and Roach heard the door to the day room closed. He waited and waited because there was no point in leaving until Sally was ready. Wandering round in his nightshirt was a sure way of attracting attention. When his watch showed midnight, Roach waited for the nurses' next check on the patients. He then tied the inside handles of the entrance door to the nearby wash basins with his shoe laces to prevent the staff opening the door should they hear him and then proceeded to prise off one of the wooden toilet seats. With this he struck the windows and cleared the shards before climbing onto the outer sill. It would have been an unpleasant drop had he fallen, but the drain pipe was within easy reach.

He listened for any cries of alarm, but heard none and slid down the drain pipe in a leisurely fashion, using the wall with his bare toes to steady his descent. The summer being a hot one the ground was warm under his feet. Although the gravel cut into him, Roach soon reached the grass verge, ignored the KEEP OFF THE GRASS notice with a smile and made his way to the gates. He had noticed the spear-headed fence when he arrived and was careful as he scaled the top; he was also grateful that he had kept on his underpants because the nightshirt caught on the spikes and ripped as he lowered himself out of the grounds of St David's.

Sally Tigg was waiting as promised, holding the roof of the sidecar open. Roach climbed in, grateful to be out of sight, Sally kick-started her Bantam and off they went. The outskirts of the town soon became countryside and Sally pulled over into a country lane, alongside which Roach saw a haystack.

"I've got your clothes in your holdall, Dave. It's best that you're dressed properly in case we should be stopped. If we are, which is unlikely, we are going to Wales to visit an aunt who is terminally ill. I'm your sister."

"Wales?"

"Nobody will find us in Wales."

"I'm sure, but do we need to go that far. I've got business here – I think."

"Your business is in Wales, Dave, near a little town called Llandrillo. I want to go on further and then we'll stop and enjoy some sandwiches that Emma has packed for us. Are you hungry?"

"No," replied Roach, "Inside, we are fed well."

"I'm starving," replied Sally, closing the sidecar and setting off once again.

When they did stop, it was two hours later and Sally found a small track that ran down the side of a recently harvested field. Leaving the motorbike, they made for the haystack and rested against some loose bales, where Sally unwrapped Emma's egg and cress sandwiches from their greaseproof paper and unscrewed the top from the thermos flask.

Roach nibbled at his sandwich, but Sally wolfed hers down in the manner Roach had seen with workmen. He watched her as she ate and noticed that she once again wore the heavy, corduroy trousers and large overcoat belted at the waist. Sally had flung the pilot's hat onto the straw when she sat, and Roach admired her auburn hair as it was tossed loose. He wondered about her age: she was one of those women who look forty in their teens but never age after that time. As he gazed at her, Sally turned and smiled with those bright, black button eyes.

"We're approaching Cambridge, and have come about seventy miles. My dear old Bantam does about 35 to 40 miles per hour, but I don't want to push her too hard. We've a long way still to go: another 200 or so miles I should imagine. It's going to be another six hours at least. Are you comfortable in the sidecar, Dave, or would you rather ride pillion?"

"I'm comfortable enough, thank you. You said you had something to tell me. Is now a good time?"

"As good as any, I suppose. I cannot see us being disturbed by the local bobby at half-past two in the morning. Let me just finish my sandwiches and have a swill of tea and then I'll begin. I was at Cambridge, by the way – Newnham College. They 'conferred' upon me the title of the degree but I was not 'admitted' *to* the degree – if you follow my gist. No? No, no sane person would. I believe it's only a few years since women were made full members of the university – '48 was it? Sorry, I'm rambling. I always ramble when I'm annoyed."

Roach waited patiently until she had cleared her mouth of breadcrumbs. When she turned to him, Roach noticed that her eyes glinted in the moonlight. *This woman was an enthusiast fixated by the need to prove her theories*, he wrote. Once she got her teeth into something, Sally Tigg wouldn't let go.

"After I heard about the Chillesford creature and knew that you had been taken off, I went to the village and asked where he – It – lived. I didn't take long elbowing out a back window to get in. There wasn't much there, but then you wouldn't expect there to be, would you, since It wasn't from this world. The cottage was more a place that the creature could pretend to call home, just to give It an excuse for being in the area. I imagine It was here to keep an eye on the base: their creature on the spot, so to speak. There were one or two devices I've never seen before and some maps, and one of these maps showed a village in Wales – Llandrillo.

Funnily enough, I know Llandrillo quite well. I do have an aunt there and we went to her house for holidays when I was a child. It's beside the River Dee near Bala Lake in the Berwyn Mountain range. Well, there are stories connected with those mountains. As a child I just thought they were spooky tales, but when I became interested in studying these space phenomena I changed my mind, and seeing that map and knowing what had happened in Rendlesham Forest, I decided that this creature from Chillesford had connections with Llandrillo."

Roach was already beginning to doubt that anything he had witnessed was true, such was the obsessive tone of Sally Tigg's voice: here was a madness he didn't want to comprehend.

"In 1947, three men were hunting along the valley of the Dee when they saw a glowing light that seemed to hover in the air and then crash behind one of the outcrops of rock. One of the men – Glyn Owen by name – went to investigate. He scrambled across the slopes, over the heather and through the gorse. When he reached the farther side of the outcrop he found a saucer-shaped craft that was embedded in the ground. Standing beside it he saw a man and a woman who, he thought, must have seen it crash. He exchanged a few words with them and said he would fetch help.

He scrambled back to his friends, explained the situation and persuaded them to come with him. They were both reluctant. When they arrived at the spot where Glyn had seen the flying saucer, there was nothing there at all: even the man and the woman had vanished. Of course, his friends thought Glyn was making it all up and once back to Llandrillo they pulled his leg unmercifully: so much so that Glyn was determined to prove he was not imagining things.

He put an advertisement in the local paper appealing for the man and woman on the mountainside to come forward. He even described the craft he had seen, stating that it was saucer-shaped with a white top and a copper underside. The underside was like a cone. The paper produced an artist's impression of the device and it became front page news for a few days."

"The silly season for news?" suggested Roach, only to receive a withering look from Sally.

"Let me finish, Dave. Glyn did more than that. The next afternoon he and his girlfriend, Olwen, cycled to the very spot. They left their bikes by the side of the road and made their way to where Glyn had seen the saucer. There was every indication that something had crashed into the earth at that place, and so they took a look around. About half a mile or so from the spot they found a creature that had crawled under an overhanging ledge of rock and was clearly in a severely wounded state. They described it as about four feet in length and insect-like with the compound eyes you find on dragonflies.

Glyn's girlfriend was – and is – a nurse, and her instinct was to try to help, but as she reached for the creature it backed off. For a moment it appeared almost human as it lay there on the ground and both Glyn and his girlfriend saw what seemed like white, downy hair on its head. But this was only for a moment. What do you do when you see a beetle with a broken wing or leg, Dave? You stand on it, don't you, to put it out of its misery? But they couldn't stand on this creature because it was obviously more than just a beetle.

A glowing aura appeared around its head and then they heard it speak like the one you met in Rendlesham Forest. Its lips did not move but they heard its voice nonetheless. The creature said that it was dying and that there was no help for it now. It would be a kindness if they carried its body to the river and lowered it into the waters when the moment came.

The creature didn't speak again but eventually the eyes glazed over and they knew it was dead. They did as it had requested, as one would grant the last wish of any dying animal. When they lowered the body into the river it was borne away in the current.

Glyn reported this to the newspaper but the report never went into circulation. It might have been that the editor considered it too improbable for words but it is more likely the newspaper was the victim of a government D notice because for days the whole area teemed with military personnel."

Sally pursed her lips, as though she didn't expect Roach to believe her anyway, when she finished her story, re-wrapped the remaining sandwiches and tightened the lid on the flask. He decided to ride pillion for a while, enjoying the night air blowing through his hair. After a further stop, during which Sally slept for an hour or so, he climbed back into the sidecar. Rough though he found the ride, Roach was sound asleep when Sally pulled up outside the Dudley Arms Hotel in Llandrillo at 11 o'clock that morning.

CHAPTER 13

Llandrillo

Llandrillo is a small village situated on the B4401 between Bala and Corwen in the old county of Merionethshire in North Wales. 'Llan' means 'church' and this is where St Trillo founded his near the River Dee in the sixth century.

Eager though they were to pursue their investigation, Sally and Roach booked into the hotel and slept until late in the afternoon. When Roach did come downstairs, he found Sally tucking into what looked like a very late breakfast. Roach wasn't hungry but sipped the cup of tea the hotel owner placed before him. He had shaved slowly in the bowl of hot water provided when he rang for service, and the leisurely shave had given him time to think. He liked Sally Tigg but felt bowled over by her enthusiasm, and had decided that whatever course of action she proposed he would follow another one, quietly. So, when she suggested having a talk with the couple who had seen the dying creature, he said he would speak with the local landowners.

"If anything is going on in these mountains surely they are the ones most likely to know about it," he suggested.

"If you wish, but I doubt whether they'll speak with you."

I have mentioned Roach's amiability before in this narrative, and it came as no surprise to me that within the hour he was seated across the hearth of one of the largest landowners in the Llandrillo area sipping a whisky and soda. For reasons that will soon become apparent, I forbear from mentioning the gentleman's name: suffice to say that his reception of Roach was both cold and eager.

"It is not for me to discredit eyewitness accounts of such events, Mr Roach, however unlikely their occurrence may seem. Both Glyn and Olwen are well-known to me – indeed, she was on hand to deliver my third child – and both are people for whom I have the greatest respect. I would point out, however, that neither of them has any desire to have this matter broached again. We had enough excitement from outsiders when – rather ill-advisedly, I thought – Glyn approached the local newspaper. Something unusual did happen on Cader Bronwen that night, but exactly what it was remains a mystery and it is best that it stays that way. However, you and Miss Tigg have come a long way and if you would like a tour of the spot where the incident occurred I am happy to arrange it for you. Shall we say tomorrow morning at 10 o'clock?"

With that unexpected offer, Roach was dismissed and driven back to the village where he bought a pint at the hotel bar and sat drinking, while waiting for the meal he had ordered to arrive and wondering how Sally's enquiries had fared. It was here that his approachable nature served him in good stead once again – much as it had at the Butley Oyster: he dropped into conversation with one of the locals who used the hotel bar as a pub. An elderly man walked across and asked if he might share his table, and no sooner had sat down than he began talking.

"I'm too old now not to be worried by silences," he said, "or to be intimidated by those who have something to hide. We need to speak out. There's too much respect for authority. There are people in this village who are afraid to vote the way they feel on election days because the local landowners are there as returning officers, dressed in their tweeds and looking stern. People are intimidated, see. You've got the local policeman on the door as well, and people wonder whether they'll find out how we voted."

"They're not socialists, then?" asked Roach with a smile.

"They're not likely to be, are they – not the aristocracy and the upper classes. The term 'socialist' is a term of abuse around here – on a par with 'bugger'."

"And you think they've a reason for keeping quiet about the goings-on on Cader Bronwen?"

"It seems obvious to me. We all know Glyn Owen's story but that's not half of it. There're lights and buzzing noises often in the Berwyn Mountains, and sometimes explosions."

"Have you ever taken a look?"

"I'm not a fool. I keep well clear of the mountains at night. On the day Glyn Owen saw the flying saucer land, we were told to stay away. The authorities said a plane had crashed and that they had it under control. But I ask you – if a plane had crashed, wouldn't there have been injuries and wouldn't the nurse and doctor have been called? But they weren't – not for a moment. The RAF had it cordoned off. No one could get near it – even if they'd wanted to. The mountain rescue team wasn't called in and the police were sent home."

"Where did the RAF boys come from?"

"RAF Valley on Anglesey," replied the old man, clearly annoyed at having the flow of his story interrupted, "By next morning the whole story had changed. It was no longer a plane crash but a meteor."

"Did these flashing lights on the mountainside continue far into the night – after the report of the crash, I mean?" asked Roach, wondering why the body of the dying creature had not been discovered while the mountain was cordoned off.

"Then and since," replied the old man.

Whether or not he might have learned more, Roach was unsure. At that moment, Sally Tigg bustled into the hotel foyer, saw him at his table and hurried over. When Sally arrived the old man clammed up and took his drink to the bar.

"Have you learned anything further?" asked Roach.

"Not from Glyn or Olwen. But they referred me to the editor of the local paper, and several things became very clear when I spoke with him. Firstly, Glyn's story of the dying space creature never saw the light of day: he confirmed that the government slapped a 'D' notice on the press preventing them from printing any further stories in the interests of national security. Secondly, he told me that most of the lights seen by the locals were centred round a place called Arthur's Table – it's a small hill on the Llandrillo side of Cader Bronwen. This is a deified spot, Dave: a place where the ancients held the equivalent of religious ceremonies, where earth energies are trapped in the rocks, where ley lines meet ..."

"Whoa, whoa – just a minute. Never mind the mumbo-jumbo: what else did you discover?"

"It's not mumbo-jumbo, Dave!"

"Let's stick to the facts. A 'D' notice prevented further stories in the press, the activity was centred round Arthur's Table – and?"

"One of the RAF men involved – a friend of the editor – told him to stay away from the spot because high levels of radioactivity had been found. He wouldn't be drawn any further on what went on that night."

"Just a friendly warning," suggested Roach, "rather like the one given by one of Guy Fawkes's co-conspirators who advised his friend not to attend parliament and so exposed the Gunpowder Plot."

Sally looked at Roach *as though I was from another planet*, he wrote, and then asked how he had got on. When he told her, Sally went to the bar and bought him his second whisky and soda that night.

The next morning the first rains of that summer fell lightly as Roach and Sally, collected from the hotel by one of the landowner's ostlers, were conveyed into the mountains by pony and trap.

"It's part of our lives," explained the man, "We wouldn't be without the horses and ponies. There are places round here where a car couldn't take you, but a pony will find its way through, even if the ride is sometimes bumpy. You'll see them in town as well. Many an old biddy goes to the shops or chapel on her pony and trap."

Roach listened quietly, allowing the ostler to ramble on. He was aware of an unease in the man he couldn't fathom and knew tension often released itself in talk. When they reached a point on the road from where the pony could no longer pull the trap, the party walked on and so came to the place where whatever it was had crashed. There were no longer signs in the grassy of the hillside: if it had been a meteor then the debris had been removed – but why, why cart away pieces of rock? Roach wasn't sure why they were there. What had they hoped to find after all this time?

"How far from here is the hill called Arthur's Table?" he asked.

"It's not much of a walk," replied the ostler evasively.

"We've plenty of daylight left if you would lead the way."

The ostler shrugged and led them along sheep tracks to the Llandrillo side of the mountain. It wasn't far – not in terms of mountain walking – and again Roach wondered why the man had hesitated. The place did not strike Roach as spectacular but Sally was electrified. She dashed around, sniffing and trembling like a dog on a scent, moving round in circles on one spot and then scuttling along imaginary lines as though tracing a spiders web on the ground.

The ostler walked away and sat on a rock with his back to Sally and Roach, and stared out across the mountainside. Watching his back, Roach realised that the man was crying and walked over to him, leaving Sally to her gyrations. The man sniffed and turned away, but Roach insisted on sitting beside him, and so he had no choice but to leave or explain. The ostler neither looked at Roach nor looked back at the hill known as Arthur's Table; he strode off down the mountainside and was soon lost from sight. Roach made no attempt to follow him or to call his name. *At that moment, I understood it was intended I should be here and that the ostler had merely been the means*, he later wrote in his diary. He turned back to where Sally was still running around like an excited child. In her hand she held a twisted, forked stick of the sort used by dowsers. It jerked as she ran.

Roach decided he only had to wait and so he sat, watched Sally's experiments with her twig and wondered. Despite all that had happened and despite the evidence he possessed in the photographs held by Emma and the remains of the Rendlesham creature's body he had kept, Roach began to doubt that any of his experiences were at all real. Looking out westwards across the mountainside towards Bala Lake, he began to understand why only a few eccentrics would attempt to fit the pieces of the jigsaw into any kind of meaningful picture. It would take a huge stretch of the imagination to link giant beetles with flying saucers, which were – presumably – spacecraft capable of impossible journeys across the vastness of space: and from where and for what purpose? It was far easier to assume that his own government and that of the Americans were involved in developing advanced aircraft to protect their national security and that sometimes things went wrong: experiments failed or produced unexpected results.

To suppose anything else, to construct other explanations, would involve him in believing that the world he had inhabited for years was under a threat that had lingered beneath the surface for, perhaps, centuries. It would involve him in accepting that an intelligent life-form was secreted on Earth and conducting experiments that would eventually change the world forever and, he supposed, for the worst. Somewhere along the line of this advance, picnics by the river, walks in the park, tea by the fireside and presents at Christmas would all become meaningless and, therefore, cease to exist. There might even come a time when there would be no more 'children' as we understand the term and, therefore, no more 'parents' and 'grandparents', no more 'courting couples', no more 'young love' , no more ... human consciousness that produced works of art. Roach wrote that he didn't know what engendered these thoughts. Perhaps they had been building up within his own mind ever since ... ever since Sir Robert's apparent lack of concern for his own children. Was that the moment when Roach had first felt the chill of a being from another world?

"You want to go away from here, sir – just go and don't ask questions. This is an accursed spot – the whole of this range, not just here."

The voice shook him from his reverie and Roach looked up at the ostler who had returned and was watching him.

"Dave," he said, "My name's Dave – not sir. Call me Dave. Why have you come back?"

The man retreated into silence once again either afraid to speak or uncertain of his loyalties, Roach supposed.

"You were meant to leave us here?" he asked.

"Yes ... I was meant to leave you here."

"On orders from your employer?"

"Yes. He trusted me to carry them out. I was his batman during the war. We go back a long way and through difficult times."

"And now you feel you're betraying him? You can go. We're meant to be here. There are questions to be answered."

The ostler removed a hip flask from his pocket, took a long drag on the contents and offered the flask to Roach, who took a comradely swig and handed it back.

"I've been hereabouts before with the master," said the ostler, "and I know who or what will be waiting for you. You know the lake to the west of here – Bala by name? That's one way they use into the mountain."

Seeing Roach's puzzlement, he continued:

"Their craft are submersible. They enter the mountain by water. Don't ask me how or exactly where, but I've seen them go down under the water – a bit like a submarine, you know – and they must pass through into some underground cavern. The master's been down with them – but he's not one of them, you understand. I thought at one time that he might be working for the government – he's an honourable man, you understand – but at other times I've had reason to wonder."

The ostler's loyalty was painful to behold as he attempted to defend what he saw as the indefensible; in the same breath he was betraying his master and protecting Roach.

"You've actually seen these craft go under the lake?"

"My son and I fish like many another. I've seen them rise from the water and sink beneath the lake."

"And you've seen your master enter one of these craft?"

"Here – on the mountain – yes."

"But you've no idea why?"

"No."

"What happened on the night when the one crash landed?"

"I wasn't involved and neither was the master. We read about it in the following day's newspapers. The mountain was cordoned off but not for long – not for as long as people make out. The newspapers had a field day for a short while."

"And so you've no idea who the couple were?"

Even as he asked the question, Roach realized that the 'couple' were simply a manifestation of two of the creatures. In the same way that he had 'seen' the gent from Chillesford, so Glyn Owen had 'seen' a couple.

"I know nothing of it. I only know I've brought the master here for meetings with them."

"You've seen them?"

"I've seen what they want me to see."

Roach realized that the ostler's terror resided more in what he imagined than what he had actually witnessed; but this was true of every sighting so far. No one had actually been harmed by these creatures from outer space, except by implication or imagination. Yet, it was generally believed that he had killed one, and Roach had no doubt that these creatures knew that to be so. Suddenly, he leapt to his feet and shouted to Sally Tigg.

"I want you to go back to the village with our friend and persuade your newspaper editor to cough up more of what he knows."

"And what will you be doing?"

"I want to hang around here for a while."

"You're wasting your time lying to me, Dave. You simply want me out of the way. I can read you like a book. Besides, the energies of this place are alive with expectation.

Something's going to happen and I wouldn't miss it for the world."

"Go back, my friend," Roach said to the ostler, "You've done your job. Look upon tomorrow as another day. Take your grandchildren for a walk. Speak lovingly to your wife. Enjoy the companionship of your friends."

The man's face was filled with grief as he looked at them, and then he took to his heels and ran as well as he could through the bracken and rough grass down the side of the mountain and away.

"Isn't this exciting?" exclaimed Sally Tigg.

Roach had no words for such a comment. He looked at the woman and decided that he had been right in the first place: she was mad.

The early drizzle that had eased off during the morning returned and was quite pleasant in the heat of the day. Roach leaned back against the hillside and lit his pipe. He was frightened and a smoke was always calming. Sally joined him, removed a cheroot from an expensive-looking leather case and inhaled deeply. Roach smiled to himself, thinking that he had never before seen a woman smoke a cigar.

"You've heard of George Adamski, haven't you?" she asked, "His space flights with the Venusian are legendary. He is among the elite when it comes to contact with people from another world."

Roach noted that he had read somewhere of Adamski, who claimed to have travelled aboard a flying saucer. Roach had no time for such nonsense and said so.

"You sneer at these claims even now – standing here on this hillside, waiting?"

As they smoked and spoke, the drizzle had become slightly heavier and was accompanied by a light mist. It was from this mist the ship descended so silently that neither Roach nor Sally was aware of its presence until they heard a low whining sound. It was a smaller craft than the one Roach had seen skim over the trees of Rendlesham Forest and it hovered about ten feet above the ground. Roach noted the dome below the craft and watched as part of it slid to one side. From the aperture appeared what might have been a beam of light or an actual, translucent tube. Roach felt himself overcome by an intense calm. *I realized,* he wrote later, *that nothing much mattered, that I was safe in the arms of these people, that I could rely on them to see to it that things were done as they should be done and that what was done was for the best and for the good of all mankind.*

The beam centred around him and he became aware of being lifted, sucked up along the beam as cash capsules were sucked along tubes in the department stores of his boyhood. He looked down and saw Sally on the ground waving frantically. He looked up and saw figures awaiting him in the hatch of the craft and the next moment he was standing beside them, calm but disorientated and with no clear memory of the moment he had entered the flying saucer.

CHAPTER 14

The Base

(Most of account in the next three chapters is taken directly from Roach's diary, which he completed later from his notes and memories of the time. Just how those memories were re-kindled will become clearer as this narrative approaches its conclusion.)

When I recovered consciousness I was lying on a table of some kind. I could not move a muscle but, glancing at my wrists, I realised there were no physical restraints. The sensation was similar to that physical experience we all have from time to time when waking in the night we appear to hear footsteps making their way upstairs but find ourselves unable to move, struggle though we might to get off the bed. As the footsteps get nearer, terror takes over, sweat covers our bodies and we fight to free ourselves from the restraints that exist only in our minds.

My natural terror increased when I realised that I was naked. I had neither memory of my captors after I entered the craft nor of my clothes being removed. The idea that some creature from another world had stripped and exposed me in this way was abhorrent to me and I felt physically sick. After a while – how long I cannot remember – I realised that I must open my eyes fully and acknowledge what was happening or was about to happen.

Standing by the side of the table were three of the beetle-like beings described by my poacher friend, Harry Cole, and similar to the one shot by the farmer, John Bird. I was aware, too, of another standing behind me and a fifth who was approaching the foot of the table with a tray of what seemed to be medical instruments; certainly, among them I saw a scalpel or two and what looked like tweezers. My horror increased when one of these creatures bent over the table and stared into my eyes. I had no belief in hypnotism, but that this being was attempting to mesmerise me was plain from its manner. To my shame, I felt unable to look away and could do nothing but return the stare. Its eyes were compound like those of a dragon fly but their focus was quite fixed. I drifted into a kind of sleep but remained fully conscious of all that was happening.

My first ordeal was to have a long tube inserted into my nostril. The tube was of some metal substance and at the end of it was a bright light, although whether this was an actual light or merely the reflection from the shiny metal tip of the probe I was unsure. But there was no doubt about the pain. If you have ever had a gallstone forcing its way along the narrow tube of your urinary tract it will give you some idea of the agony I experienced. I hated myself for screaming out as I did, and loathed myself even more when I looked up at these creatures and begged for mercy. Four pairs of those strange eyes returned my look (the fifth was behind me) but with no expression of compassion. I convinced myself in desperation that their eyes were unable to express emotion, and realized later that this was the case. I also doubted that they had feelings as we understand the term.

The pain subsided as the probe was withdrawn and I gasped for air as the sweat rolled from my body. I struggled but could not move.

The light in the room then changed from stark white to a mellow orange glow, and I felt surrounded by warmth and comfort. At first this was a relief. I began to breathe more easily and looked around. The creature behind me had not moved but was cradling my head in much the same way as a nurse might do. The creature with the tray of instruments had moved to one side at the foot of the operating table and a third had placed itself in a standing crouch position and was making some adjustment with its claws between my legs. Imagine my horror when I found myself being sexually aroused. Something was being attached to my genitals and I was aware that I was about to ejaculate. When I did, there was a sense of excitement and release followed by an immediate loathing that this act, which I had always anticipated to be associated with gentleness and love, was brought about by such vileness. I was angry and wanted to cry – indeed, I may have done so. I had been abused and I was humiliated and helpless; but then, with a sudden pain, the pressure on my genitals eased and something was removed, and to my disgust I felt eternally grateful to these creatures.

I lay still for a bit – again how long this was I have no idea – wondering what further afflictions I was to suffer. After a while, I dared to open my eyes and look around. I could hear that the creatures were still in the room because of the dry, rustling sounds made by their movement but I could not see them. My head was still held immobile but I swivelled my eyes in all directions. It was a round, white room and above me were a battery of lights the like of which I had never seen before: they seemed to comprise a series of round circles the size of the silver threepenny bits my mother put in her Christmas puddings, but there were no bulbs or floodlights as we know them. These had now been turned down and glowed feebly; my hopes that my ordeal was over mounted.

I soon discovered that in one sense it was but that another of a more subtle kind was to follow. The table on which I was prostrated began to move and I was wheeled – if wheels were the means of propulsion – across to the other side of what I must now see was the equivalent of one of our operating theatres. I felt my body lifted in a floating motion from the table and steered towards a large semi-circular tunnel. The creatures did not seem to be raising me. It was more like the conjuring trick when the magician on the stage has a human body apparently suspended rigid in mid-air. There were no hoops to prove the absence of wires: just a sense of being levitated and guided towards this device. I almost laughed, picturing how I must look.

Once inside the tunnel, I felt no pain but I was conscious of being explored. Within the confines of my prison an arc of light slid back and forth over my body as though taking photographs. I suppose it was carrying out similar procedures to those undertaken by our X-ray machines but in a considerably more complex manner. After a while, I was inserted further into the tunnel until my head emerged at the far end.

One of the creatures was waiting with what I can only describe as the skeleton of a helmet. At first I thought I was about to be electrocuted, but there were no wires attached to this helmet and I managed a sigh of relief. The feeling of being examined and probed and tampered with was still strong within me and it was all I could do not to vomit. My gorge rose and a powerful sense of nausea overwhelmed my whole body, as the creature arranged another machine over the helmet and I heard them connect with a whirring sound. What happened at that moment is beyond anything to which I can relate to give an image of what I experienced: suffice to say that I felt my brain was being kneaded like dough. Only whereas the ingredients of dough are brought together by the fingers of the cook here the ingredients of my mind were being prised apart. There was no pain in the way we understand pain, but a sense of sheer terror. I thought, quite literally, that these beings were taking my mind to pieces: that once they had finished with me I would exist no more.

When I woke – because I must either have fainted or been put to sleep – I was alone and no longer in the operating theatre, and someone – or something – had replaced my clothes. I felt groggy and afraid to attempt any movement, but this sensation did not last for long. Once I realised that I could turn my head I did so and eased myself to a sitting position. Whatever had happened to me had left me as weak as I have ever felt even after a day's walking in hill country. Although feeling was returning to my legs and arms, I could barely take my weight as I tried to swing my legs to the ground. I sat for ages hoping my strength would return. I was hungry, of course, because I hadn't eaten since breakfast in the Dudley Arms Hotel. Dudley Arms Hotel! What and where the hell was that, I wondered: light years away, another lifetime in another place? Fear stalked every muscle and every fibre of my body. I ached with fear. If fear can be said to be able to take over a body, it took over mine. I trembled with fear; it drove me to the verge of suicide. I was desperate to make a move and equally unable to do so. Hours seemed to pass before I could force my feet to touch the ground and badger myself into a standing position.

When I did so all thoughts of suicide left me because there was simply nothing in the room that could be used for an act of such atrocity. The room was devoid of anything but the shelf on which I must have been placed. It wasn't simply that it lacked furnishings: it lacked everything. Such light as there was seemed to emerge from the walls and ceiling, which were curved and featureless sheets of metal. There wasn't even a door, let alone a door handle. They must have got me into the room, of course: that I realized. I asked myself how. Was there a panel in the wall? If so, it was invisible. Nothing to see and nothing to give me support as I struggled to walk. I made my way round the room, leaning heavily against the walls, one of which suddenly opened; it seemed to lift outwards and then slide to one side. Half-expecting one of the creatures to enter I waited and then the door closed in my face; but as I lurched forward it opened again and I stepped swiftly from the room into a corridor.

The corridor, like the room, was curved and, also like the room, without features of any kind: no doors, no air grills and no lights. Still dazed from the tortures I had suffered, I made my way to the right. I was aware that I would appear to be escaping and equally aware that I must not seem to be doing so.

These creatures must breathe, I reasoned, and therefore there must be air vents to the surface. The surface! Yes, I must already have decided that I was no longer on the spaceship that had collected me from Arthur's Table. The whole place in which I was imprisoned was too large for it to be part of that particular ship. Then, I reasoned, they must have brought me down here, perhaps through the lake as the ostler had suggested. Where was Sally? I had last seen her waving frantically as I drifted upwards to the spacecraft. Had she been brought, too?

I sat down in the corridor and wept silently. If I couldn't order my thoughts I would never escape, and my thoughts were scrambled. Why had they brought me here? Why had I wanted to come?

The place – let us call it the creatures' base – was so silent ... and airless ... and without sunlight. One of my uncles had served in the submarine service during the war, and he had commented on how the lack of sunlight used to frazzle the nerves of crewmen and on how relieved they were to get out on deck. I felt like that now, trapped here in this underground world. He had said that the best submarine crewmen had a placid temperament and a steady nerve; this stopped them getting on edge. Sitting in that corridor, I remembered his words with gratitude and, after a while, stood up more quietly determined than ever.

Eventually, I came to a panel in the wall that looked as though it might separate from the rest and open as the one in my cell had done. I stopped by this panel and waited, but not for long. It seemed to know I was there and it slid outwards and along. Steadier now and ready for what I might find, I entered the room. Picture your science lab at school but without the wooden bench tops, the sinks, the rows of test tubes, the Bunsen burners, the bottles of chemicals, the shelves of equipment, the rubber tubes, the gas taps and so on, and you will see this room in your mind. It was clearly a laboratory but without the clutter; everything to be used had been secreted within the walls behind glass or plastic windows: everything including the specimens.

I had never liked the idea that parts of animals should be preserved in jars for us to gawp at. Call me foolish if you like, but it seemed to me to lack respect for the living and the dead. I would not have made a good scientist! I was once shown the embryo of a stillborn child preserved in this way and it disgusted me. What I saw now filled me with equal loathing: within one of the walled containers were at least fifty tanks, each one containing the embryo of a human being or that of one of the space creatures immersed in a greenish liquid.

I knew from my science master that the young of some insects, such as dragonflies and grasshoppers, did not look very different from the adults; whereas in the case of beetles and butterflies the young did not look anything like the adults and were usually referred to as grubs or larvae. The embryos in the tanks were very like their adult version. Remembering their compound eyes, I realised that the species I was up against were not to be thought of as insects in the way we understand the term (looks deceive, as my mother warned me) but the embryos advanced my knowledge not a jot. The gent from Chillesford had talked of a third species and what he called the 'thread of life'. All these embryos told me was that something unpleasant was in hand, and I knew that already.

I was about to leave this laboratory when I heard that unpleasant rustling sound behind me and knew I was being watched. One of the space creatures had entered the room and was observing me closely. It was my first chance to take a careful look at one, and so we stood without communicating for a longish time, neither one of us in any apparent hurry.

The creature before me – who I had every reason to fear but in whose immediate presence I maintained a defiant calm – looked like a giant insect. Its body was divided into three parts – the head, the thorax and the abdomen – and the three pairs of 'legs' were attached to the thorax. The head contained the mouth, the eyes and antennae by which it must both smell and hear for I saw no suggestion of ears or nose in the face. It was *the eyes, of course, that held my attention. I had seen these before as one of their medical team leaned over me when I lay on the operating table. They were compound and set quite apart almost on either side of the head. I could not imagine them missing movement of any kind. The thorax was covered with a large, leathery plate, which I took, at first, to be armour but later realised was the creature's actual skin. Its legs protruded from the thorax: one pair downwards and two upwards, so that it seemed to have four arms. These appendages seemed to have four parts: one that attached each leg or arm to the body, a femur, a tibia and a tarsus. The latter part consisted of five short segments; on the lower 'legs' these formed a foot and on the upper 'arms' they formed intricate claws. The abdomen ended in a pair of short growths rather like the pincers on an earwig. I wasn't sure what the function of these might be but later learned that they grasped the female during the mating process. It seemed to be wingless and the skin was a deep violet for most part but with a black sheen along the sides and on the chest.*

The creature was the first to communicate; its thoughts appeared in my head, and the mouth did not move.

"We thought to dispose of you, Roach, for the killing of our companion, but were mistaken. Which was the bird?"

I wondered what it knew. Had someone told it of the gent from Chillesford's death or had it learned that from the scrambling of my mind; and what had it learned? Had it seen the killing or did it simply know of it? If it had simply read 'bird', in John Bird's interests I had no wish to disabuse it.

"It was an accident," I replied, picturing an eagle as quickly as I could.

The creature paused, clearly puzzled and I was frightened that an image of the farmer had appeared in my mind. I saw the blue and black carcase on the ground and held the picture in my head.

"We have taken samples from you and you are marked. You will go now."

"One moment," I replied, "I need to understand. Samples? Marked? What do these words mean?"

It's hard to communicate with a face that holds no expression; words alone convey little. I thought I may have guessed much but I needed to know. Suddenly, I did not want to leave this place.

"Who are you?" I asked, "Where are you from? Who was the ... man who was killed?"

"Why do you ask these things?"

"It's called curiosity," I replied.

It looked at me for a while, perhaps unable to comprehend what I wanted, before turning to the door and beckoning me to follow. We proceeded along endless corridors, all as barren of furnishings as each other, until we came to yet another door that slid open along the wall. I entered another room without features and watched the creature I had followed communicate with one who must have been some kind of superior. Its swivelling eyes examined me for a while, decisions passed between the two and I was led away to a further room.

This was as bare as the rest but the walls were home for various screens. These were completely different to those of the television sets some of us bought two years ago to watch the coronation of Queen Elizabeth: they showed coloured pictures and were much slimmer, fitting into neat slots on the wall. I was left alone to watch these screens for a while but the pictures meant nothing to me; some seemed to convey images of a dead world, while others were clearly places on our planet, Earth. As I watched, I heard the door slide open and turned to see what appeared to be a man. He was tall, blond and wearing a one piece outfit made from a metallic substance. I could not help but smile as my guess become knowledge.

"There's no need for that," I said, "I am beginning to understand and seeing you as you really are will help me no end."

Immediately the image vanished and before me stood a creature similar to the first and clearly of the same species.

"*Our visitors usually find the image more reassuring,*" said the creature.

"*But you actually remain the same, do you not? You only appear to look different?*"

"*Yes.*"

"*Your companion who was accidentally killed chose to convey the image of an old, rather eccentric man because it fitted the public house scene?*"

"*That is so. It allows us to move more freely among you.*"

"*You project the image to our minds as you are projecting your thoughts at this moment?*"

"*Quite so, Roach.*"

So the '*children*' who had played with Norman Bird had not been '*children*' at all. The words of the farmer's son came back to me as I listened: '*His clothes were different ... they were ... light ... they didn't seem to weigh nothing ... I grabbed at his jacket and it was so light it wasn't there*'.

"*You wish to know about us?*"

"*Yes. I need to know. I need to make sense of what is happening to me.*"

Did I see the semblance of a smile in the strange eyes? I don't know. The creature's claws took hold of me and I was guided to a bench that slid from the wall. He seemed to know I was tired and weakened by the operations performed on me so recently.

As I sat, I caught sight of the mouth, which was huge and dominated the whole of the lower part of the face, I wondered how and on what these creatures fed.

"*Flesh, Roach. We must have fresh flesh,*" it said, catching my thoughts and adding, as it sensed my repulsion, "*Like your own species. We will eat any living thing.*"

It must have touched something as it spoke because, unexpectedly, a large screen – larger than any screen imaginable – appeared from the wall.

"*That was our planet and its place in the Solar System (I will use your terms) was an orbit somewhere between your* planet's and that of Mars. You will know that the further a planet is from the Sun the older it is: so, Venus is a younger planet than Earth and Mars an older one. Our planet, therefore, was older than yours when we resided on it and we are an older civilisation than yours. Hence we were and are more advanced in technology. You are wondering what our planet was called?"

"Yes." I replied, feeling slightly pathetic at being concerned about something so relatively trivial and annoyed that it knew.

"Our name is not pronounceable in your language. Since your scientists have named the planets after Roman gods, shall we do the same and call our home Minerva, after the Roman goddess of wisdom?"

It did, then, have a sense of humour I thought.

"It is only captured from your species, Roach. I am merely imitating what I hear. Perhaps you might refer to us as Minervans?"

I smiled and the Minervan's eyes sparkled. When they did it was like watching a rainbow dancing.

"Many centuries ago, our home planet was threatened by a huge asteroid. It was far larger than any known to you. The asteroid Gaspra is the largest in the Asteroid Belt, is it not, and measures a mere nineteen kilometres across. The one that was on line to collide with Minerva was four times that size. We knew that our planet would be driven off course and spin away, eventually burning up in the darkness of outer space, when the collision occurred; but we had anticipated and we had time. We had by that date built colonies on our moons and on Mars and so we were able to plan an evacuation. A vast spaceship was built – what your people call a flying saucer – and the superior ones among us were chosen to leave Minerva. Mars was a dead world by then and our colonies were supplied from Minerva. Mars was dependent on Minerva – it could not function independently, you understand – and so we turned out attention to your planet, Earth, which was *much younger and fertile and fruitful as ours had once been. And so we came and established our bases."*

"Bases?" I queried.

"You do not imagine that this is the only one, do you, Roach?"

"I've never given it a thought."

"No, and that is good. We have survived here a long time because of your people's scepticism about our existence, but we have not flourished. The experiments have taken longer than we had hoped to come to fruition."

"Experiments?"

"We could have conquered your planet, Roach. We could have attacked and razed it to the ground, but what would have been the outcome? We would have inherited a dead planet, and we needed life. Our species and yours can co-exist but in secret and with difficulty. The only real answer to our problem – and yours – was to produce a third species."

"The thread of life?"

"Yes, and that needed experimentation to bring it about. You would like to know more?"

"Like isn't a word I would have chosen," I replied, and the rainbow eyes sparkled again, "but yes I would like to know more."

"So that you can escape and expose us," suggested the Minervan.

I smiled, damning myself for allowing him access to my thoughts.

"That will not happen, Roach, for reasons that will become apparent. But come, I am pleased to explain and to demonstrate how much we have achieved. And you can reacquaint yourself with Sally."

"Sally's here?"

"Yes. She was younger than we thought and so we brought her, thinking she would prove of use."

CHAPTER 15

Thread of Life

Sick with terror I stood and followed it from the room. My horror was not centred solely on what might have happened to Sally but on the implacable tone of the Minervan's thoughts and my fear about how far the experiments of these creatures had progressed. The Hargreaves children were home – I knew that to be so – but how changed were Patricia and Myles? Were they any longer human?

The Minervan leader – I took him to be so because of his aura of authority – led me along curved corridors to yet another sliding panel and yet another featureless room: featureless, that is, except for Sally who sat on a ledge, similar to the one on which I found myself when I woke, eating what appeared to be raw fish. She looked up as I entered and the relief on her face was rather flattering.

"Dave! Oh am I pleased to see you! Don't ask. I'll talk when I'm ready."

I sat beside her on the ledge and she pressed close against me. For some reason, I hadn't expected this reaction from such an independent spirit, but it was a joy to know that I wasn't alone in my fear.

"They did horrible things to me, Dave – I can't tell you ... They inserted a long filament into my ... I'm a virgin – I expect you know that ... I'm sorry. I do need to talk this out of me."

While she cuddled even closer and I felt the trembling from her body, one of the Minervans entered with a dish of the raw fish and placed it before me.

"It's not so bad," laughed Sally, and it was some comfort to hear her laugh, "They've treated it with something similar to vinegar. It's not unlike that cold, Spanish soup ... gazpacho, do they call it?"

My distaste for my breakfast seemed to relax Sally, and she proceeded to talk about her ordeal.

"I felt this tube moving around inside me. It was extremely unpleasant. It seemed to be searching, and then I realised that it was probing my fallopian tubes ... fiddling around inside my womb. The pain was unbearable when it reached me there, I can tell you. I screamed. I've never experienced such agony in all my life. These creatures don't seem to know about pain, do they? Have you noticed that fact? They looked down on me and I felt they were puzzled. Perhaps their nervous systems are different to ours. Perhaps they don't have one. My screams didn't stop them in what they were doing. I think I fainted with the pain ... When I woke I was alone, and my clothes were placed on a shelf at the side of the room – neatly folded they were. I was almost amused. I got dressed and wandered about the room in a daze. Eventually one of them returned and brought me here ... What happened to you?"

I told her of my own experiences and all I knew about the Minervans while Sally finished her meal and mine.

"What can they mean by a third species? They can't imagine that ... that's unthinkable," she said, horrified at the image crossing her mind.

I didn't know. She was an intelligent woman, and so there was no point in offering her a soothing but meaningless opinion. We sat silently, holding each other to give solace, and waited. It was a relief when the door finally opened and I recognised the Minervan who had explained about the destruction of their home planet. It beckoned with a gentle wave of two of its arms, and Sally and I followed it to another laboratory.

If the first could be described as unpleasant with its tanks of embryos, this one was even more so: the tanks were filled with abortions, floating once again in that green liquid. Creatures that were part human and part Minervan stared us in the face. How such monstrosities had come into being does not bear thinking about, but there were many of them, all failures – we learned – of early experiments.

The Minervan directed our gaze to a large screen set into the wall, over which it ran its arms. Images appeared. It was rather like being in a lecture hall, and – in a way – we were. There was pride in the creature's manner. Human egg cells – vastly magnified – appeared on the screen and within each we saw what both Sally and I recognised as the gent from Chillesford's 'thread of life'. It was, indeed, a thread of sorts, and his image of milk straws constructed into geometrical shapes was an apt one. As we watched, a metal filament appeared, probing and plucking until it removed one strand of the thread, which was then replaced with another.

"Now you understand, Roach?" asked the Minervan, as it garnered my memory of the gent from Chillesford's image, "Within each species there is the thread of life. If we remove any parts of your thread and replace it with parts from the thread of another species we would produce a separate species that would have many of the characteristics of both parent species, but it would be quite distinct."

"And this new species would be perpetuated in any offspring?"

"Yes."

We watched as the offspring perpetuated made their way across the screen, each experiment culminating in a violation of both parents. I find it difficult to portray what Sally and I saw on that screen. Imagine Darwin's Tree of life on which someone has re-located the branches so that the characteristics we associate with our insect world have progressed further along the main trunk, bypassing the fish and the reptiles and the birds and the primates to become re-united with the characteristics of our own species – man. A multitude of images presented themselves, and all were horrific.

"All failures, Roach, until we learned that what was needed was subtlety; that is, the combination of not physical characteristics but essential characteristics. Eyes on legs and arms projecting from the thorax were leading us nowhere but to a hideousness that would provoke a violent reaction. If our species was to survive in your world it would have to look like your species but encompass those distinctive qualities that made the new species Minervan in outlook ... Yes, we would have to cease to exist in order to survive. Minervans like myself are the ones of the old order."

Looking back from our early twenty first century perspective it is easy to smile at Roach's lack of understanding, but in 1955 what appeared before him and Sally Tigg on that screen seemed nothing more than the work of the Devil or, at best, the work of some deranged species intent on creating monsters. The creature obviously read this thought in Roach's mind at that moment because it continued:

"You may be repulsed by the nature of our experiments, Roach, but compare them to your own species' attempts to survive and multiply. When one of your races wants power, it goes to war against another, annihilating millions in the process. Forty thousand were slaughtered on the battlefield of Borodino alone to satisfy the ambitions of the race you call French. Our way does not adversely affect the balance of power on Earth and nor does it undermine your institutions. Such changes as are necessary for our survival will come about gradually through the actions of enlightened individuals. We are here to bring about a New Age for your species and for our own."

"You're meddling with nature," Sally cried, "You're interfering with God's work."

"Nature has always meddled with itself. Mr Darwin taught you that simple fact. If it were not for Nature's meddling, your species would not exist."

I was surprised that the thought planted in Sally's mind was also in my own, and the Minervan captured my puzzlement.

"We have a collective intelligence and a collective memory, Roach. What I know of you and what you have been told is known also to my companions. Similarly, we share each other's thoughts. I know, for example, that you have wondered about the possibility of escape. There is no need. As you were told by my confederate, we shall return you to your world now that we are finished with you."

My thought was stifled in a moment but, once again, the Minervan caught it.

"No, Sally will remain with us for a time," it said, "There is work to be done."

"Then I will stay, too," I replied.

The compound eyes looked me over. The creature knew I was making the offer only to plan an escape for both Sally and me. Did those rainbow eyes sparkle? I don't know. I was only aware of the awful fact that there was little chance of an escape from this place: the Minervans would know every thought that passed between us.

It was fortunate that we were both returned to the cell Sally had occupied: she was able to confide her fears even if, as it seemed, we could share no plans of escape.

"What do they want with me, Dave? I'm forty years old. What did they mean by probing my fallopian tubes? What possible interest can my egg cells hold for them?"

I have never felt so helpless in my life. This was to be my first defeat and one of many but always, always it was my worst. It is a terrible thing to have to listen to someone in mortal fear and be able to do nothing. Sally knew that in some way her body was to be taken over for their purposes: were her egg cells to be removed, or had this already happened? We talked over the frightful images we had seen on the screen and the abortions enclosed in the green liquid. The idea that part of her was to be used to further the Minervans' ambitions was appalling to Sally. I have never met anyone tougher in spirit than Sally Tigg, but she wept on my shoulder until it was soaked with her tears.

In the calmness that followed, as we sat close in mutual comfort, I became aware that my mind was occupied with how we might plan an escape. Could I block thoughts from the Minervans by holding one in my head and another on my tongue? My mother had always claimed to be able to think of several things at once and I had known her hold a conversation with our neighbour while planning what we were to have for lunch. Perhaps I could emulate her?

It was while these thoughts passed through my mind and we sat together on that wretched little shelf that the door opened and all hope faded. I knew they had come for me and so did Sally. Had I been John Wayne, it would have been so easy: I would have slugged my way out. But there was no chance for such a manoeuvre and no point. Where would we run? Neither of us had any idea of where the lake might be in relation to our prison or where the air ducts might lead – if, indeed, there were any air ducts!

Sally clung to me and screamed as the Minervans approached, and something must have snapped in my mind. I struck out, foolishly and pointlessly and – possibly – harming our chances of consideration. The Minervans were slighter in build than us and less stable in their movement. I floored three of them in the cell before they realised what was happening and sent the fourth spinning into the corridor. We were free! I grabbed Sally's hand and we ran. We had just reached the bend in the curve of the first corridor when something seemed to strike me on the neck.

When I woke, Sally was no longer with me and I was lying on my back on the floor of the flying saucer that had brought us to the Minervans' base. Two of them stood by me, their implacable eyes watching me for any aggressive movement. Eventually, the dome beneath the craft slid to one side and a beam of light shot earthwards. Once again I was overcome by that intense calm as I was lifted into the light and felt myself drawn through the air. My stomach heaved as it might have done on a helter-skelter. I was dropped suddenly as though rejected by the beam of light and found myself struggling to extricate my arms and legs from the bracken of the hillside. Above me, the space craft hovered for a moment, spinning round its centre, and then shot skywards before disappearing.

It was nearly dark. I had lost Sally and was miles from anywhere or any help. Excuse my panic! I sat down. There seemed nothing else to do. I had to collect my thoughts. If only I had seen the direction in which the saucer flew I might have had some sense of where I was since I knew that Bala Lake lay to the west, but it had simply vanished. Behind me were the hills and valleys and before me a slope that must lead down to a river if not to a road. That seemed the sensible way to go. It was a ragged descent through tussocks of wet grass and boggy patches of ground. In places I was knee-deep in rough grass, and in others my feet sank into the small mires of the hillside. I could see nothing but this kind of terrain for miles; there was not even a sheep to break my feeling of being isolated from the world. My one hope lay in the rippling sound of the occasional stream.

Eventually I came to a knoll from which the ground fell steeply. Faced with the need to return the way I had come or risk twisting an ankle I decided on the latter course and began to pick my way gingerly towards what I hoped might be a river. Once there I would follow its downward course and, hopefully, make my way to civilisation. I was soon leaping from tussock to tussock trying to avoid the bogs and hoping my feet would land on solid earth. Usually they did but the risk of a broken ankle remained a permanent worry until I arrived at the edge of a mountain stream. I was quite exhausted by now and grateful for a drink of the icy water.

The edge of the stream was littered with stones that made the going rugged but I was making better time now that I had left the hillside and my hope was that I could raise some help and organise a search party. The ostler had seemed a decent man, if under the control of his master, and I had this vague hope that he might know more than he had told me about the

Minervans' base. If he had seen one of the craft enter the lake then he may well have some idea of where we might locate the entrance.

I had been running and stumbling for a couple of hours and it was now much darker than when I had been dumped. Still I saw no road before me and the stream seemed to be threading endlessly through beech and elder trees. Somewhere ahead there might be a road but how steep would be the valley sides down which I must clamber? I wondered whether my best bet might not be to jettison my reliance on the stream and head along the ridge. This would take me back into the hills some way but the going might be easier.

I took a seat on an old stump to catch my breath and realised with an enormous sense of relief that my pipe and tobacco were still intact in the side pocket of my jacket. It may now sound pathetic that I was so relieved to have a smoke, bearing in mind what might be happening to Sally at that moment, but I was and it calmed me down immensely. I had been running wildly and it was time to take stock of my situation. Ridge or stream – what was it to be? If I reached the end of my pipe without it going out, I would take the ridge; if not, I would follow the stream. I have since discovered that major decisions are often taken on such a whim.

Ten minutes later I was making a steady ascent of the ridge, leaving the tree-lined valley slopes to my left. In less than half-an-hour I was abreast of the ridge and before me, perhaps a mile across open country I saw a ribbon of road, white in the moonlight. It had to lead somewhere and I decided to make straight for it. Rambling in hill country is never a matter of 'straight', of course, but I kept as near to that desired aim as I could: I had no intention of losing sight of that road now that it was located.

My RAF days had kept me fit and, despite the nature of my predicament, I found this final stretch of my escape enjoyable. Beyond the road was a series of hills, and the moonlight picked out, even at that distance, the white shapes of sheep grazing.

This was another homely sight because sheep meant a farm nearby, and so I hurried on. The inevitable piece of moorland soon replaced the ridge and I lost sight of the sheep for a while but the stars were out by now and one, whose name I did not know, held me on my course. The stars and planets had always been a mystery to me and the universe a place of wonder but, as I struggled on what I supposed to be the last part of my journey, I was minded of Wells's comment that 'we can never anticipate the unseen good or evil that may come upon us suddenly out of space'. How right he had been!

Crossing this wretched piece of moorland, I doubled my pace. A fear lurked within me that I might rise from it only to find the road had disappeared, and I felt, foolishly, that speed would prevent this catastrophe. Eventually I reached its further limits and found myself climbing yet another ridge which led me across a stretch of bracken-strewn pasture and so to a long dyke. This I part-clambered over and part-splashed through: by now I was desperate for the road and the wet bothered me no longer. Beyond the dyke lay a further stretch of moor lined on one side by a row of trees and on the other by a stone wall. Ignoring the fall of stones, I climbed the wall onto a rough road. Someone had pounded small stones into the potholes of what had been a track and so made a highway accessible by farm cart, and I could see hoofmarks in the softer ground. Farm carts meant a farm! I blessed my sheep and hurried on.

Turning a corner bounded by a copse of beeches, I came across not a hill farm as I had expected but a large house. Why I had not seen this before I could not imagine. The only explanation was in the lie of the land: coming as I had from lower ground, first the ridge and then the line of trees must have screened the residence from my eyes. It didn't matter to me. Here was civilisation and that meant help.

I opened the gate and made my way across a roughly-cut lawn bordered by rhododendrons. The front door of the house, which must have been the residence of a well-to-do farmer, was approached by a flight of seven steps placed between two imposing lions. I noticed a telephone cable running from a pole near the gate to the house, and then down the wall into one of the front rooms. So, whoever owned this property was on the telephone. My hopes rose.

I mounted the steps and pulled the handle of the bell. Its sound reverberated in what I supposed to be a capacious hallway. While I waited, I noticed an archway leading from the side of the main building; through this I glimpsed a courtyard and stables. When the front door was opened, I saw that the hallway was cluttered with boots, walking sticks and some leather harness. The smell of this permeated the air; it was reassuring and pleasant in its homeliness. The man who stood facing me was clearly the master of the house: his whole manner suggested authority and ownership. He greeted me with a smile.

"It's not often we receive strangers at this hour, my friend. Come in and welcome."

It was the traditional greeting of the countryside, and I had no doubt that I would be offered some refreshment. Again, as I realised how hungry I was I thought of Sally and felt guilty.

"You're clothes are quite wet," said the man, whose smile broadened as he spoke, Have you come far?"

"I've been crossing the hills for some hours," I replied, "and I have a strange story to tell. I need help fairly urgently. A friend of mine is out there somewhere and in the deepest trouble."

"I'm quite sure that is not the case," he replied, ushering me through the outer porch and into the hallway proper, "Let's find you some dry clothes, some food and drink and then we can talk. You're lucky it's a warm night. The summer has been kind to us."

His tone was both soothing and knowledgeable, and inspired immediate confidence. Freshly clad, with a whisky in my hand and a tray of bread and cheese before me I looked closely at my saviour as I began my tale. His was a kindly face, burnt red by the winds of the Welsh hills. As he puffed on an old meerschaum, the smoke rose before his snub nose and passed by a magnificent pair of bushy eyebrows towards the high ceiling of the room. The light from a table lamp caught his friendly expression; the smile was in his eyes as well as his mouth, and it was these eyes that I noticed for the first time. When the man smiled, they sparkled, and it was like watching a rainbow dancing.

CHAPTER 16

Man from the Mountain

I knew at once that I had walked into the home of an adversary, and he read the thought before it could be stifled.

"Enjoy your food, Mr Roach, you have nothing to fear from me," he said, and as he spoke I noticed that his mouth moved.

This wasn't, then, an illusion to reassure me: this farmer was an actual man, rather than a creature. He watched me, and read the bewilderment as much in my eyes as in my thoughts. He smiled and nodded at the food.

I'd had enough. I hadn't eaten for goodness knows how long and I was exhausted by my hike across the mountain. I swilled down the whisky and he refilled the glass. As soon as the first piece of soft bread and butter touched my mouth, I was ready for the next and for the beautiful Welsh cheese that had been placed on the small table at my knee. For a time I didn't care about anyone except myself. All I wanted was to eat and sleep.

As I wolfed down the food, I became aware of other sounds in the house: sounds exaggerated by the silence in the room. I heard what sounded like a woman's voice and the chatter and laughter of children.

"My wife is putting the children to bed," said my host, refilling my glass for a second time.

A wife and children! Did he say a wife and children? My head was swimming with the whisky, and the good food was making me drowsy. It was a fight to stay awake, but I did not dare fall asleep.

"*Why not sleep, Mr Roach? Sleep if you wish. You're not going anywhere – at least for a while. You need have no concerns for your friend. She is in good hands.*"

I became angry. He was reading my every thought and I was, to all intents and purposes, his prisoner. Besides, his tone suggested a lack of concern for Sally.

"*No lack of concern, Mr Roach, but an acceptance of what must be. Sleep if you will and, later, we will talk and you will understand.*"

To my shame, I dropped off. How long this sleep lasted I do not know. It was still dark when I woke. The food had been cleared from the table and the farmer was standing at his window looking out into the night. It occurred to me to wonder whether this man – or whatever it was – could see in the dark. Can beetles see in the dark?

Without turning, he asked if I wanted a cup of tea and left the room to fetch it when I answered in the affirmative. A crazy idea came to me that I might just walk out, but my common sense wasn't so far gone as to make the attempt. When he returned it was with a huge brown pot of the darkest and strongest tea I have ever drunk, and my host joined me before leaning back in his armchair. He laced both our drinks with several spoonfuls of sugar and the sweet brew revived me.

"*I'm Gwynfor Evans, and my family have farmed here for generations,*" he said, stretching out his hand across the table.

I accepted the greeting with some trepidation but his hand seemed normal apart from a slight leatheriness in the texture of the skin.

"*Dave Roach*", I replied, "*but you know that already. They've told you my name.*"

"*The thought occurred to me ... You are wondering where I stand in this matter, aren't you, Mr Roach?*"

"*Yes. I am beyond being simply bewildered.*"

"*It's really quite simple. Many generations ago several of my ancestors were taken by those who live under the* mountain. Quite what went on there, we're not sure but when they were returned all seemed normal, according to the tales passed down through the family. It was in the children that the differences occurred – in the children and then in their children and so on. This is all family gossip, you understand? Half-whispered tales: nothing more. No one likes to admit that they're different, but we are. You noticed my eyes, didn't you, and the way I caught your thoughts? We all have that. It's a great asset when market day comes, I can tell you, knowing what the buyers are thinking. I'm telling you this because you and your friend are in the same boat, and it helps to understand what's going on."

"Have you ever been …?"

"No – never been there and never want to go. They leave us alone except for the odd occasions like you getting lost. They'd expected you to return to the Dudley Arms, you see, and were worried. They'd kept track of you and realised you were heading for my farm. It suits them to have someone on the ground when things go wrong. Otherwise they leave us alone and we get on with our lives."

"Just a minute! Kept track of me – what do you mean?"

"I can't answer that question, but they knew where you were."

"Do you know what will happen to Sally?"

"How can I, Mr Roach? I'm not party to their business. All I know is that she will be returned. They have shared that thought. And to forestall your next question – no, I have never seen them. The nearest we came to that was when one of them was injured on the night one of their craft crash landed on the mountain. There was much activity that night and, for a while, we expected to be told to find him. But, in the event, Gwyn Owen and his girl did that the next day, according to them, that is."

I realised that I was speaking to one of the third species the Minervans had been trying to create, and Gwynfor caught the thought.

"You're wondering how we're different, Mr Roach?"

"I'm sorry. I do apologise."

"Not at all! Curiosity never did anyone any harm. Excuse me."

He walked over to the sitting room door and closed it. Perhaps his wife had reservations, I thought.

"She does, Mr Roach, but people get used to anything in time. When Sian came into the family, there were certain things she had to be told. It's in the children that the differences first become apparent, and it can be quite frightening if you're not expecting it. The skin stops shedding when we reach maturity but it's a bit startling for the children when it first happens. Some children can shed their skin up to a dozen times, but usually it's about four or five. The outer skin becomes brittle and peels away, but not before a new, softer one has grown underneath. I noticed you paused slightly when we shook hands. You had noticed the leathery nature of the skin hadn't you? Leathery it may be but we very adverse to cold and some of us are quite dormant in the winter months."

He smiled as I caught the humour in his voice. His species wasn't the only one that tended to lay low during cold weather.

"For us," he continued, "it would be better if the planet were warmer. Even in summer we find it trying ... And food – yes food! We have voracious appetites."

I didn't have to ask the question, which saved my embarrassment.

"Anything – cooked, raw or dead. Some of our neighbours find this repulsive and so we warn the children to be vigilant when they're at school. We do have a strong affinity for the natural world. Dark nights are nothing to us so long as they're warm. We hunt in the lake and none of us has ever had to be taught to swim."

He talked on, and it was interesting enough but he sounded as any man might when talking of his family's prowess. How could he have behaved differently? They were his children and he loved them, whatever changes may have been imposed upon them by the meddling of the Minervans.

But what was his attitude to other species – to me! Was he as conscious of my difference as I was of his? When push came to shove, what moral constraints guided him? Did he share the Minervans' view that they had a right to experiment with another species and adapt it to their purposes? Was he conscious of terror and pain in others? Did he have any sympathy for the common good of all mankind, or did he see only what was best for his own ... species?

Whatever made him different had come down through the generations. Traits are inherited and passed on the through the family, but there is a huge diversity within one family. Our children resemble us but are not identical. Whatever had happened to Gwynfor's ancestors would show centuries later in his grandchildren's grandchildren, and so on. Would the part of him that was Minervan be exaggerated or understated in those to come? If exaggerated, then Gwynfor's descendants would be more Minervan than human! But how did this fact help the Minervans? Surely, they couldn't modify the egg cells of a sufficient number of us to make any worthwhile difference to their race in the long term.

That was as far as my thinking went at the time, and Gwynfor had no answers. His business was farming in the Welsh hills and if his children were different to others then that was something they must get used to and, if necessary, hide.

When daylight came, I shared a large breakfast of smoked fish from Bala Lake with him and his family and then he gave me a lift on his pony and trap to the Dudley Arms Hotel, where I hoped to find Sally. Gwynfor and I parted on the best of terms, but my sense of unreality deepened and I was filled with a terrible foreboding the precise reason for which was beyond my understanding.

Roach was to wait several days before Sally was returned. He abandoned any idea of forming a rescue party after a conversation with Glyn Owen, who convinced Roach that he would be wasting his time since no one would believe him. He prowled around the town but the only person who offered any new information was the landlady of the Dudley Arms. She told him that after the strange craft crashed into the mountain a group of men had arrived at the hotel.

"Commercial travellers we're used to, but these weren't commercial travellers. Posh they were – all of them. Spoke quite la-di-da, if you know what I mean. They made several trips backwards and forwards to the mountain, but never told anybody what they were doing there. Close – that's the word for them – close."

"How did they get there?" asked Roach, hoping there might be someone who could provide him with further information: someone who owned a pony and trap, perhaps.

"They arrived in their own car. I think my husband said it was a Morris Oxford. Attracted a lot of attention they did, but kept themselves to themselves."

"Men from the Ministry?" suggested Roach.

"They certainly worked together. They were very comfortable in each other's company, which is just as well since they didn't welcome ours."

"You never overheard any of their conversations?"

The landlady looked at Roach as though he had overstepped the bounds of decency in asking such a question, but responded nevertheless.

"They always retreated into silence when I approached their table with food or drink but I did notice that their notepaper was always headed with the letters APEN."

"You've no idea what that meant?"

"No ... I did hear them once talk about an agent. I had the impression he was a local man. I heard the words 'field officer' and they mentioned some pieces of equipment – a strobe something. Would that be right?"

"A stroboscope! Yes. It's a lamp that flashes intermittently. They're used by engineers to enable them to see the movement in machinery that's rotating at speed."

"They also talked about teletapes – whatever they might be."

"It's a way of passing on information. We used it in the RAF," he said, and then added, as an afterthought in his diary, *although not where I was based in Sharjah where we still relied on Morse code.* "Thanks for your help. It's been most useful."

"It's time I locked up for the night now, Mr Roach. Would you like another brandy?"

"No thank you. I'll get to bed myself."

"Don't worry about your friend. She'll turn up. They always return."

As he undressed for bed, Roach realised that he had, indeed, stopped worrying about Sally. Realistically, he had no chance of reaching her and both their fates were now in the hands of the Minervans. Despite this mental stance – the only one he could adopt to retain his sanity – he was raddled with worry to the point of desperation. He wrote in his diary that night: *I felt helpless in the way one feels helpless when a beloved pet is dying and there is nothing – simply nothing – that one can do. I have never felt so low in my life. This feeling of impotence is overwhelming; it is a terrible thing to have one's fate in the hands of your enemy.*

Lying in bed, he heard the landlady closing the outer door: the large key he had noticed hanging over a small bureau in the foyer made a distinct noise in the lock. Another door closed and he heard her foot on the stairs.

Roach had dozed off – not asleep but engaged in fitful dreams – when he was awoken by a bright light shining in through the window. He jumped from his bed, crossed to the window and flung back the curtains. Hanging in the air about ten feet above the street was a spherical object that emitted a light, part blue and part white. He shoved up the sash window so that the bottom half was open and peered out. The object pulsated but he saw no movement within it. Angry for reasons he couldn't explain at that moment, Roach left his room and made his way down the stairs to the front door, which he opened with the large key. All fear seemed to have left him in his burst of anger and so he stepped out onto the pavement. A tube of light extended itself from the object, and Roach became aware of a ringing sound. This was felt rather than heard and soon his body was pulsating in rhythm with the sound. It was a sickening sensation. He closed his eyes and gulped down air as rapidly as he could. He seemed to move and he wasn't sure whether or not his feet left the ground. When he opened his eyes again, he saw Sally floating down from the object along the tube of light and he was rising to meet her. Soon he had clasped her firmly in his arms, and they were both standing in the middle of the road. Looking up, they both saw the strange craft as it was for the first time. The bright light faded as the craft moved away, and they saw what looked like a large wheel, the spokes of which ran to a spherical hub. The lights along the outer rim flashed blue and white for seconds and the Minervan craft shot up into the dark of the sky. Soon it was nothing more than a twinkling star. Roach turned to Sally.

"Well, at least they gave you a lift home," he said, and was relieved to find that she found his quip funny. "Let's get inside and brew you a cup of strong, sweet Welsh tea."

Sitting in the hotel kitchen gulping down cup after cup of Roach's brew, Sally said nothing for the best part of half-an-hour and Roach was sensitive enough to respect her reluctance to talk. When Sally did speak it was only after she had taken his hand and held onto it like grim death.

"What have they done to me, Dave, what have they done? I'm an old spinster. I'm not going to have children at forty, am I? What can they have wanted to achieve interfering with me? I have been assaulted by these creatures and I hate them. I've never hated anything in my life until this moment, and the feeling is not a pleasant one."

Roach listened and wondered. They had come all this way from Suffolk and achieved nothing other than to be treated as specimens. Why had they come? To find out more, he supposed. Looking at Sally he felt a kind of revulsion. It was only for a moment, but he couldn't deny the feeling. How was she changed? Was this the same lady who had arrived at The Oyster on her motorcycle, ordered a pint of bitter and astounded the locals?

Sally looked at him through eyes that were normally strangers to tears but now wept copiously. He could see that she was not aware of what he was thinking, and was relieved and grateful. *At least*, he wrote, *she was still the Sally I could lean on and trust.*

"Do you feel any different, Dave?" she asked, and it was the first time he had thought about himself in quite that way.

"Eh, no, I can't say I do."

He told her about Gwynfor Evans and the generations of change the Welsh hill farmer's family had experienced. As he talked he remembered Gwynfor's remark about him being 'tracked', but Sally was as puzzled as Roach.

"I'm so tired, Dave. I need to rest. Let's stay here for a day or two and then make our way home when I feel fit to drive. Tell the landlady to let me sleep in tomorrow. I'm ragged with exhaustion."

It was, in fact, three days before Sally felt fit to mount her Bantam and drive off on the long return journey to Suffolk. Roach sat pillion and the wind blew through their hair so that Sally's auburn mane caressed his face.

CHAPTER 17

Return to Butley

Life in the village was so normal that it was unnerving. Emma and George welcomed them back with a rabbit casserole

"I'm sorry," said Emma, "I'd no idea you were coming back today. It's just a rabbit that Mr Cole dropped off. I'd have done something special if I'd known."

"This is special enough for us, my dear," replied Sally, "and the stock is superb."

"Oxo," laughed Emma, as they sat round the little table in the kitchen.

"A little Oxo in the casserole improves it out of all proportion," laughed Sally, quoting an advertising slogan of the time.

Emma told me forty years later that there had been a tension in Roach and Sally on their return. She sensed that they both felt constrained, and so she chatted amiably about nothing much while the meal progressed from rabbit casserole to a plum duff covered with Birds custard.

"The grocer, Mr Geater, has a van now," she said, "Not that it's much quicker than the delivery boy going round on his bike, but he's very proud of his van. I place the order when I go into Woodbridge and he insists on delivering it. I could easily bring it back on Mr Catchpole's coach but he insists on bringing it to the door."

"Perhaps it's that glass of home-made lemonade you charm him with!" laughed George.

And so the conversation drifted. Summer was coming to an end and "hadn't it been a glorious one"; Rachel and Tom

Ward had at last been allowed to go up to the big house and play with Myles and Patricia; Geraldine Hargreaves – both relieved and frightened on the return of her children – had been over to Creek Cottage and seemed grateful to have spent time with Emma; Harry Cole – "not usually the world's greatest conversationalist" – had been round to talk with George several times bringing Reggie with him; it had been a good harvest and "the Harvest Festival would be on us sooner than we realise"; everything had been quiet at the American air force base; George was looking forward to going back to school ...

"What about you, Roach? Are you taking up Sir Robert's offer?" asked George.

"I haven't decided," replied Roach, aware that, unusually, he and his cousin had not strolled into the garden for a smoke while the women cleared the table and did the washing up. "Perhaps it's time we told you of what's happened since Sally rescued me from the asylum?"

Roach and Sally, during their several rest breaks on the journey home, had decided what they would, and would not, tell George and Emma. Roach was all for sharing everything but Sally was more reticent: reluctant to go into any details of the experiments the Minervans had conducted during their time on Earth. Leaving these details aside, they related the whole of their experiences in Wales.

"So these ... animals are conducting some sort of breeding programme," said Emma, not having been blinded by what she had not been told.

"Not as we know it," replied Sally, "At least ... yes, not as we know it."

"You mean not as we do – man and woman?"

"We don't know about that side of their lives. Presumably they must reproduce their own kind under the mountain, since those who first came – God knows how many centuries ago – cannot have lived forever ...," explained Sally.

"... but that is quite apart from what you have just called their 'breeding programme'," continued Roach, relieved that

Emma was forcing them not to beat about the bush. "These experiments are aimed at producing this third species: the best of us and the best of them."

"It's not a joke, Dave," snapped Sally.

"Sorry ... I'm trying to understand what they hope to achieve by putting bits of each of the species together."

"And what they are doing is far, far more subtle than 'putting bits together'. The Minervans have experimented towards the biological possibility of combining the characteristics of two species to produce a third. Remember the gent from Chillesford's analogy of the horse and the donkey producing the mule, which possesses the best qualities of both parent species?"

"Yes," replied Roach, quietly, "with infinite patience and a clear sense of purpose they are proposing to produce a species that will inhabit our world successfully."

"And will this new species supplant us as the dominate one – eventually wiping us out as we wiped out Neanderthal man?" asked George, "Perhaps there's not much point in us having children after all?"

"Don't be silly, George," said Emma.

"We don't know the answer to that anymore than we know how they hope to achieve such a scheme successfully. As I said, they cannot possibly adapt the egg cells of vast numbers of human beings: that is, the world's population."

"What are you two going to do?" asked Emma.

"An appointment at the Home Office to see a minister might be a beginning," replied Sally, "and then we shall investigate further."

"You have physical evidence of what you are saying?" asked George.

"Some of the remains of the creature I shot, the photographs Emma kept for me and whatever they have done to ... me," replied Roach.

"And Sally?" asked Emma, catching the significance of Roach's pause with the acuteness of a woman's intuition.

"Yes," replied Sally, in a decisive tone that indicated to Emma she had no intention of allowing the conversation to continue much further. "Perhaps we should clear away while the men have a smoke?"

Roach was still laughing as he and George, leaning on the latter's new gate, lit their pipes.

"Sally eager to clear away the dishes," he chuckled, "How uncharacteristic ... You and Emma have taken in all we had to say without a murmur, George. I take it, then, that you believe us?"

"Why shouldn't we?"

"Because I'm not sure that I believe it myself. Had you spun me such a yarn when I arrived a few weeks ago, I'd have put it down to your living in the countryside."

"What I do find hard to believe is the one-time existence of their planet, Minerva."

"The name was suggested with a touch of humour," replied Roach, "but it will do, and I don't see the problem with that notion, at all. My astronomical knowledge is crude but, as I understand it, Earth is about 100 million miles from the Sun with Mars at about 150 and our other neighbour, Venus, at about 70. We – that is, Earth – are at just the right distance for the temperature to be perfect for water to exist as a liquid, whereas Venus is too hot and water only exists as vapour if at all, and Mars too cold and water only exists as ice.

But this cannot have always been the case, can it? The Sun is cooling down. At one time it must have been sufficiently hot to have created the right temperature for water to exist on Mars, just as one day it will be sufficiently cool for water to exist on Venus. By which time, Earth will have ceased to exist as a habitable planet.

Water is the source of all life – I think Darwin said that life began in the seas and swamps. If you have water, you have the chance of a breathable atmosphere. It seems quite credible to me, therefore, that Minerva – orbiting the Sun at somewhere between 100 and 150 million miles distance – could well have supported life forms long before the Earth was able to do so.

Our planet has been threatened many times with destruction by passing asteroids. Is it not conceivable that a particularly large one destroyed Minerva, but was anticipated by those living there who, consequently, planned an exodus for the favoured few?"

"Yes, I suppose, it is." answered George, "One theory advanced to explain how the dinosaurs suddenly disappeared from Earth is that we were struck by a large asteroid running amok in space."

The two men stood silently after that little discussion. Eventually, without consulting each other or mentioning their intention to the ladies, they walked to The Oyster, lighting their second pipe of the evening on the way.

The landlord looked up as they entered and poured their "usual" with a nod towards their usual seat. Roach thought he might do well to forget what had happened and settle down with a cosy little wife to raise a family in this village. He didn't think the Minervans would bother him again as long as he kept his nose out of their business. He could find work in Woodbridge or perhaps Ipswich and see out his three-score-years-and-ten in peace and quiet. Harry Cole coming over to speak with him only concreted that belief in his mind: that is, until he saw that Harry had Reggie with him. The little terrier wagged its tail for Roach, who leaned down and gently rubbed its sternum. It was at the moment he remembered the Cairn's terror on the night the space craft had landed, and Roach accepted, without commenting on the fact to George, that his destiny was already decided and he had no chance of settling anywhere.

"You'll be going to Sir Robert's fete, will you, Mr Roach?" called William Ward from the bar, "My wife would be pleased to meet up with you again. She's certain you had something to do with the children returning."

"Fete?" queried Roach, "I thought ..."

"Later than usual," explained George, "but Sir Robert insisted and Lady Hargreaves has commandeered Emma's help in organising it ... What are you laughing at?"

"Nothing," replied Roach, "except the resilience and perversity of the human spirit."

The Hargreaves' fete was in full swing when Roach and Sally arrived, although Emma and George had been at the hall since early morning: Emma to assist Geraldine Hargreaves and George to run errands for Emma, who had found her country niche and was now in her element, as she told me all those years later.

Sir Robert and Lady Hargreaves had done their research as far as village fetes were concerned and their event, intended to raise funds for St John the Baptist church and to establish their credentials with the villagers, embodied all that was traditional and best in English village celebrations. There were processions with the participants decked out in white shirts or blouses with white gloves and green sashes and a young girl from the village was crowned queen of something or other; mock auctions – reminiscent of the real thing at one time – were held in which husbands offered their wives to the highest bidder; tables were laden with the home-made bounty of the village and with beef now 'off the ration' several joints of this held pride of place alongside a hog roast and an abundance of fresh summer vegetables; the landlord of the Oyster supplied barrels of a light ale called Summer Pride; butts were set up on a far lawn for archery; a bowling green invited the old men to lounge on its sloping banks; elsewhere the sound of mallets hitting croquet balls could be heard; there were obstacle races and egg-and-spoon races for the children and jugs of home-made lemonade to cool them off; picnic clothes were spread; there were wrestling matches for the young men and quoit throwing for the women; and there were craft stalls where such arts as skipping-rope making could be learned.

Roach – a townie at heart – was dazzled by the plethora of goodwill and activities, and Emma, apparently forgetting their fateful conversation of the previous day, led him from stall to table to sporting event as though none of them had a care in the world; even Sally, probably the more troubled of them all, was persuaded to try her hand at archery.

"Mr Roach, it's good to see you have returned safely from your Welsh jaunt. How do you like our little summer fete – later than usual, unfortunately, but hopefully welcome none-the-less," hailed Sir Robert when either he or Roach eventually managed to track the other down.

Roach found himself being steered towards a quiet corner of the rear terrace of the hall where Sir Robert's manner changed immediately. He poured a large whisky for each of them and sat Roach down as though he were a Dutch uncle about to advise a young nephew on the foolishness of a romantic attachment.

"Sit still, Mr Roach, and clear your mind of this fete. Think Llandrillo and let your mind roam over your experiences of the past week."

Roach looked up from his drink at the other man and observed his eyes for the first time: they sparkled, and it was like watching a rainbow dancing. He wrote in his diary that night: *I had known all along, of course. Nothing else could explain the man's composure when his children disappeared. But like everyone else I refused to believe what was, quite literally, staring me in the face. And now I sat watching him as my very memories were absorbed and analysed. I didn't care. At least it would save my having to explain. At the same time, I was terrified.*

"Naturally, I had been informed of your escapade, but the details eluded me and, to an extent, still do. I think, perhaps, you know more about our friends than I do, Mr Roach."

"Friends!"

"How else can we look upon a superior race whose technology is able to advance our own world by centuries rather than decades?"

"As our enemies?"

"I think not. They have avoided a conflict in which they would, undoubtedly, have fared far better than us, and chosen to live and thrive among us as allies."

"Allies consult each other!"

"Come, come, Mr Roach. That was hardly a realistic course of action for our friends. Instead, they chose to combine the talents of our two species into a third, which will, eventually, make a far better job of ruling this world than we have managed to do. My family, like your Welsh hill farmer, benefitted from the successful outcome of earlier experiments – not, I might say, a word that appeals to me greatly – and through my children these benefits will become greatly enhanced, as will the benefits to their children's children and so on."

"You mean that the future generations of your family will become more and more Minervan and less human?"

"Ah – Minervan! I quite like that nomenclature, Mr Roach. Was it your idea?"

"No, it was a touch of humour on the part of our ... friends."

"Don't hesitate when you use the word, Mr Roach. Already they are beginning to adopt some of our own characteristics."

"It's intended to work the other way, though, isn't it? What I don't understand is how you could remain so calm when you knew what was happening to your children back there in the base of these creatures."

"It was necessary to determine just how far the adaptations had progressed."

"And they came down through your side of the family, and not Lady Hargreaves?"

"You're very astute, Mr Roach."

"Your wife was distraught."

"Yes ... My wife has no Minervan blood. It was not a marriage of which they – our friends – approved ..."

"... because had you married another of your kind, the adaptations would have progressed more rapidly?"

"Yes. You only breed successful racing pigeons by a careful selection of the stock you allow to mate. Likewise, with hunting dogs: those that continue to produce successful off-spring …"

"We're not talking about bloody dogs or pigeons!" Roach expostulated, "These are your children!"

"Exactly, Mr Roach – you have it in the proverbial nutshell. The children of the future: the third species."

"Those people like you and Gwynfor Evans are … halfway houses, so to speak?"

"We'll make a diplomat of you yet, Mr Roach."

Roach sat in silence, and Sir Robert made no attempt to interrupt the flow of his thoughts. Combined with the knight's sense of humour there was a detachment from the realities of the Minervans' enterprise, a coldness that allowed Sir Robert to both love his wife and children and yet, at the same time, see them as small cogs in a vast machine. Roach could not imagine himself adopting such a stance – such a pose – in the face of the reality he envisaged. Yet, if Mr Darwin was to be believed, and Roach did believe him, we had all progressed, by a random process he called 'natural selection', from the amoeba of the primeval swamp – through the stages of worms, crustaceans, fish, insects, reptiles, birds and the vast array of mammals – to the apes and man. Millions upon millions of years had passed to attain that emergence. What had taken Nature so long to achieve, the Minervans were attempting to bring about in centuries through 'unnatural selection'.

It seemed to Roach, as he sat sipping Sir Robert's whisky on the terrace of Hargreave Hall and listening to the jollity of the village fete, that the only course of action open to him was to beg re-admittance to the lunatic asylum.

"That was an unfortunate occurrence, Mr Roach," explained Sir Robert, "but we had to keep you quiet, if only momentarily, because events seemed to be getting out of hand."

"It also had the advantage of branding me as a loony forever," replied Roach, "Whatever I might say, do or write from now on can always be explained in that way."

"Yes," agreed Sir Robert, without demurring from the brutal truth, "You appear to consider the randomness of Mr Darwin's theory to be quite acceptable, if I might say so, but object to the more scientific approach of the Minervans."

"Random is one thing," answered Roach, "Coldblooded something else."

"Would you not rather our destiny be decided by benign scientists than left to the whims of nature? Our planet will become uninhabitable one day, and all man's achievements will perish unless we make decisions now that will avoid the catastrophe."

"Even if I agreed with such a preposterous notion, I don't understand," said Roach, "how the Minervans hope to populate the world with their third species."

"They don't have to do so, Mr Roach. They have but to adapt the world leaders."

"The politicians?"

Sir Robert laughed, a hearty and human laugh, as he replied:

"Politicians may come and go, but civil servants go on forever ... Don't look puzzled, Mr Roach. Countries – all countries – are led not by politicians but by their civil service. I mean, of course, the senior civil service and not the bureaucrats you meet in the local offices. And the senior civil servants are for the most part recruited from the principal public schools in this country or 'private schools', as they are called, in America and elsewhere. All countries are ruled by the educated elite of which I am a member. Many governments – such as those in India and the Far East, for example – rely on the skills of people educated at Harrow, Eton, Benenden, Cheltenham Ladies College and so on. To move the world in the desired direction, all one has to do is to select children from those institutions: Over a number of generations the necessary adaptations will produce leaders favourable to the Minervan cause."

"And you have bases such as the one at Llandrillo all over the world."

"Precisely. World leaders do not emerge randomly, Mr Roach, but by careful selection, however unnatural ... I am not *asking* you to join us, but *urging* you to do so. There is more to this venture than the creation of a third species. It offers us rapid and vast advances in technology that will be manufactured by people such as you who will gain – as will the whole world – from these developments. You are used to life in the service of your country and your skills in the fields of wireless and photography will be beneficial to our work at De Havilland where we intend to engineer the aircraft of the future."

"You're not telling me that De Havilland is run by Minervans?"

"De Havilland is run by the most respectable people in the country, and the government is eager to encourage their work through grants, which ..."

"... you are in a position to allocate."

"Precisely."

Once more, Roach sat in a state of bewilderment, desperate to establish for himself the parameters of his likely conflict, to distinguish between friends and enemies. He ran his mind back over the events that set him on the path to Llandrillo: Agnes Ward's tale of the children's disappearance was followed by the road block – the road block and the sentry ...

"The crash at the American base was an accident," said Sir Robert, cutting into Roach's thoughts, "We visit occasionally for technological reasons. Certain members of the base are familiar with our desire to develop advanced aircraft and are eager to assist ..."

"There was a coffin," interrupted Roach, "I remember the long box – the one that reminded me of a munitions box ..."

"You have ... a keen eye ..."

The uncustomary hesitation was enough for Roach. He caught the evasive look in the knight's eye and smiled.

"Yes," said Sir Robert, "it was what the papers like to call a flying saucer and, yes, one of our allies was injured ... killed. It was necessary to facilitate repairs to the craft and ... see to the removal of the body ... Key members of what passes as their civil service and their military are among our number, and military personnel know how to obey orders. Indeed, they have no choice. Besides, by now those servicemen involved that night will have been disbanded as a group and posted to other bases around the world."

"Having been suitably de-briefed," said Roach, emphasising the last word.

"As you say ... There are no sinister 'goings-on' – to use the vernacular – but merely a genuine desire to serve one's country to the best of one's ability. As a serviceman yourself, you will understand that perfectly, I am sure. Think about my proposal, Mr Roach. I'm offering you the hand of friendship."

CHAPTER 18

Dominant Species

The fete was still in full swing when Roach sought out Sally Tigg. He was aware that he had just undergone a thorough de-briefing: he knew everything but could divulge nothing because no one would believe a story so fantastical, and he was reassured that all was for the best in the best of all possible worlds. He also knew that he could play a part in the great endeavour: that would be the sensible course of action. He would only be a small cog in the great machine – smaller even than Sir Robert's children – but his part would be vital, he would receive a decent salary, a guaranteed pension and the occasional pat on the back. Working among fellow enthusiasts, he would soon lose any sense of guilt because he would have no one with whom he could discuss his fears, no one who would believe such a tale; indeed, if he related it over a lunch-time drink in the local he might gain the reputation of being a great storyteller or even a noted comedian.

All this crossed his mind as he looked for Sally, who he found in deep conversation with Lieutenant Colonel Pat Humphreys. The American greeted Roach like an old friend, his charm only enhanced by the Englishness of the occasion.

"Mr Roach, it's good to meet up again. Miss Tigg has been telling me of your adventures in Wales, a part of your wonderful country with which, I must confess, I am unfamiliar. It seems that you have both been having an unusually exciting and bewildering time."

The man smiled so broadly that Roach felt he couldn't but agree with him; at the same time, following Sir Robert's urgings to join the cause and secure the future, Roach felt himself tipping, once again, over the edge of reason. Perhaps the asylum was the best place for him? Perhaps there he would find peace and freedom from this one-sided fight. He caught the look in Sally's eye and held back the outburst that was welling up within him. Eventually, the American excused himself and strolled off amiably into the grounds.

"We're not alone, Dave. We will find allies."

"Where? I've just had a long talk with Sir Robert. I'll give you the details later when we're away from here, but the gist of the matter is that anyone of any importance who is in a position to influence the governments of the world is already seeing things from the Minervan standpoint or will be before long."

"But there must be many who aren't. I said we should go to the Home Office. My family have one or two connections in Whitehall. I know someone who will listen to us."

Roach's heart sank. Could he really believe that to be true?

The garden fete remained lively until late into the day. It was only when darkness began to fall that the craft stalls wound up their materials, picnic clothes were folded into baskets, bowls were bagged, mallets no longer cracked against croquet balls, arrows no longer swished into butts and what remained on the tables of food was carried home, singing voices faded into the distance and Roach and Sally wandered back to the cottage with Emma and George.

Sitting in the little frontage that would one day become a garden at Creek Cottage, Roach related all he had learned from Sir Robert and Sally outlined her intention to travel to London within the week and seek help from a family friend who worked in the Home Office.

"Geraldine Hargreaves seems to have accepted the situation," said Emma, following a long silence during which they sipped the lemonade she placed on the little table they had carried from the kitchen. "Her attitude is, quite simply, that Myles and Patricia are her children. Whatever may have happened to them, they will always remain part of her, and she of them."

"Yes," replied Roach, very quietly, "that is true. But I find it hard to believe that anyone could accept such a situation."

"What choice has she, Dave?"

"No choice. I can see her predicament."

The darkness deepened as they sat and talked. All four were only too pleased to place the information they held outside themselves; a trouble shared was certainly a trouble quartered. Roach kept struggling with knowledge he held but had half-forgotten – something the landlady of the Dudley Arms Hotel had mentioned: the strange men, the papers on the table.

"APEN," he said suddenly, "have you heard of a group called APEN/"

"No," replied Sally.

(Sally was later to come across this group, although she never met any of its members, all of whom treasured their anonymity. She did discover that the initials stood for Aerial Phenomena Enquiry Network. The group seemed to appear suddenly at critical moments, especially during the 1970s and 1980s, and then to disappear just as suddenly.)

"What I cannot and do not believe," said Roach, "is that any reputable politician knows about the Minervans and their attempts to create a third species."

"Hear, hear!" George concurred, "Neither do I. Our parents' generation has just fought a war to rid us of Fascism – that is, life under the rule of those who think they know best – and many of our present politicians fought in that war or were responsible for engineering its outcome. You're not telling me that such people are going to be happy about living in the reign of a bunch of giant beetles."

Emma and Sally laughed: it was a reassuring comment, but Roach remained troubled.

"What I can't get out of my head," he said, his voice almost a scream in the night, "is that we know it is happening and why. There's almost a sense of inevitability about it – a rush to acceptance and destruction. These creatures don't care about our civilisation. They don't care about Shakespeare and

Mozart and going to church on a Sunday and *Workers' Playtime* on the radio and school outings and harvest festivals and holidays at the seaside ... everything that makes up the daily pattern of our lives."

"We need to keep our heads, Dave. There's always hope," said Sally.

"I hope you're right," he replied, "I just wish it didn't rest in me and you and people like us who might want to oppose these changes. I just wish it resided in something less tenuous. It isn't going to end harmoniously, is it, with us and the third species living side by side in peace? Once they've gained the upper hand, this third species is going to want to re-organise the world to suit them rather than all of us.

No one is attacking them. No one is setting out to stop their experiments. We run from them, we hide from them or we support them. There's no escaping their gradual but inevitable supremacy. In the end, they will look upon us – the human species – as we look upon the animals of the world: there for our convenience. They seem to favour fish at the moment but who knows when their tastes might turn to meat – and we're meat, or will be to them. Perhaps they'll herd us in fields as we herd cows and sheep and pigs. Perhaps they'll put us in cages in some futuristic zoo so that their kind can come and stare at us and poke our favourite foodstuff through the bars so that we gibber and grunt. Ever thought about that? They communicate by transferring their thoughts from one mind to another. They'll be no more speech, and those who do speak will be the oddities – something good for a laugh. And no more speech means no more words – no more books, no more plays, no more musicals to entertain us at the cinema: no more *Singin' in the Rain* or going on a *Roman Holiday*. No more cinema, no more theatre, no more concert halls, no more ... I'm sorry. It's all getting to me. I'll try and pull myself together."

"It's all right, Dave," said Emma, coming to him and putting her arms around Roach's shoulders, "It's all right."

"Yes," he said, grateful for her warmth, "Yes, it's all right."

He wrote in his diary that night how he felt ashamed at having upset Emma. She and George had every reason to look forward to a life together. Here in Butley they would raise their children, and their children would go to school and church and be part of a loving and caring community. They would eventually become grandparents: Emma fondling her children's children on her lap and George tossing them into the air and catching them. She would teach the girls to keep house and cook; he would teach the boys to hunt and fish. Whatever might be rumbling beneath the surface would not affect them for generations to come; but, eventually, the world would change and it wouldn't be for the better. No superior species had ever lived in equality with another: the one would always dominate.

"The photographs I took," he said, "do you have them?"

"I have three sets," replied Emma, with a broad, self-satisfied smile, "Call me cautious!"

"You've a wife in a million," said Roach to his cousin, as he stood and hugged Emma, "I'll take two of them: one for me and one for the minister. You keep the third set – somewhere obscure."

"And the remaining specimens of the carcase?" asked George.

"I'll take part of the shell I retained. Perhaps you'd preserve the rest, George? Again – somewhere out of the way?"

"I'd like a few more days before we leave, Dave," said Sally, "After what Sir Robert had to say about senior civil servants, I think we need to go above their heads. Daddy served in the Royal Navy during the war on a destroyer. He never said much about it (they didn't, did they?) but I do know that his commanding officer was someone of importance, and you know what these naval types are like – they remember the men who served under them. I'll send Daddy a telegram from the village post office and I hope he'll be able to arrange a meeting for us."

The eyebrows of all three of her listeners had risen at Sally's use of the word 'Daddy'. Being polite people, they didn't smile, but it had amazed them to realise that they actually knew someone who called her father 'Daddy'. *But it wouldn't be just anyone who would have gone to Cambridge*, wrote Roach in his dairy, and he realised there was more to Sally Tigg than eccentricity.

When the telegram boy arrived, smart in his blue uniform with its red piping and pillbox hat, it was with the news that the meeting had been arranged for the day after tomorrow in London. They were to wait at Liverpool Street Station where they would be met.

"What did you tell your father?" asked Roach.

"That we had some information concerning strange craft and a threat to the nation and needed to discuss the matter with a statesman rather than a civil servant or minister. We felt his commanding officer might be the person."

Roach refrained from offering to share the cost of such a telegram, fearing it would embarrass Sally, and contented himself with arranging their train to London, Sally having decided that her motorbike might prove more of a hindrance than a help in the city.

The following day, Nathan Catchpole's coach took them to Ipswich, where he dropped them at the station having left his regular customers at their usual stop on St Margaret's Plain.

CHAPTER 19

Dossier

When their train pulled in at Liverpool Street there was no mistaking the man who was waiting for them: the cut of his jib marked him out as a non-commissioned officer of the Royal Navy, probably a CPO. His smile was welcoming and brisk, and without a moment's hesitation he led them to what Roach decided was a Rover parked at the immediate entrance. The police officer who stood by the car nodded briefly to the naval man who opened the rear door smartly and waved both Roach and Sally into the rear seats; the smell of leather wafted across as the door opened and they sank back into the luxury of the ride.

The premises to which they were taken Roach assumed was a private members' club, but he later had no idea of where it might have been situated in the city. The streets around were composed of the kind of houses that stand back from the pavement, secure in their own grounds, surrounded by a low wall topped by railings and entered through a gate. The façade was a classical portico and Roach just had time to admire the symmetry of the building before Sally and he were ushered through the front door and guided along various hallways until they came to a room clad with wooden panels and furnished with leather chairs. Their guide knocked sharply twice and on the command from within opened the door and vanished from sight.

The man who rose as they entered must have been all of six feet four inches tall. To describe his posture as erect would have been an understatement: shoulders back, chest out, chin up was the order of the day. His head was large and patrician with a long nose and a wide mouth that was pursed firmly over a broad chin. The forehead, too, was broad and the hair was brushed back precisely, and Roach just knew that not one strand of it would stray. The man's eyes were a shade of blue-grey, icy cold and unflinching. Here was someone who would neither welcome his time being wasted nor suffer fools gladly. Roach recognised him from photographs in the newspapers but never recorded his name in the diary or anywhere else. As he extended his hand, first to Sally and then to Roach, a smile broke the severity of his face, but it was a smile that was as much business-like as friendly.

"Miss Tigg, I am pleased to meet you. I knew your father well. He was a fine officer and a real gentleman. I was proud to have him under my command. We saw some decisive action together. Mr Roach, I hear you're not a naval man but volunteered for the RAF to complete your National Service – Eastleigh in East Africa and Sharjah on the Persian Gulf. From the sublime to the ... less sublime, I believe."

It wasn't a question, but a statement to put Roach at his ease and let him know that the man before them was familiar with Roach's service record, brief though that service had been compared with his and Sally's father. Despite himself, it impressed Roach that this man should have taken the trouble to find out about his postings and how they differed, but attention to detail was a hallmark of the one-time naval officer, all-time statesman.

"Please be seated. It's almost lunchtime. Would you like a sherry? Now, how can I help you?"

The invitation to sit and the offers of a drink and help were all completed in one smooth movement; before Roach could draw breath, he was relaxing in the largest and most comfortable armchair he had ever experienced, sipping the largest sherry he had ever held and talking. The statesman made no attempt to interrupt but sat for almost two hours as first Roach, and then Sally and finally both of them related their story from the disappearance of the children to Sir Robert's talk with Roach at the garden fete. All the while, those cold grey eyes never flickered from an examination of their faces, while the statesman sat with his fingertips touching and his legs placed exactly with both feet on the floor.

After they had finished, he sat watching them, without speaking, for what seemed a long time. Roach looked into the eyes and noticed a faint smile; the eyes sparkled like ice in the sunlight, but Roach felt it would have taken a very brazen rainbow to dance within them.

"Thank you," he said, eventually, "your accounts could not have been more lucid. You say that you handed over the pieces of carcase to the working party who interviewed you?"

"Yes," replied Roach, "They said they were attached to the Ministry of Defence and would report their findings to the Directorate of Scientific Intelligence and Joint Technical Intelligence Committee."

"I see. Do you have any more specimens?"

Roach reached into the bag he carried and handed his piece of the shell to the statesman who turned it over several times and then placed it carefully on a side table before asking Roach whether he possessed any further examples.

"Yes," replied Roach, knowing there would be no point in lying to this man, "I also took some photographs," he continued, feeling impelled to confide fully.

"And did you also give a set of these to the working party?"

"No, I did not," replied Roach, handing over a set of the photographs he had taken with Emma's Kodak Box Brownie.

"Perhaps you felt the need to hold something in reserve," said the statesman with a smile, "One does not always know with whom one is dealing ... These are most interesting, Mr Roach. You wouldn't by any chance have a spare set would you? I would like to keep one for myself and another for this working party could prove useful."

"Take these," urged Roach, handing over his second set of prints, "Unless you would prefer the negatives."

"Yes, the experts might well prefer the negatives. I have always found these people to be most suspicious, especially when faced with the possibility of an unpalatable truth. Keep the second set for yourself, Mr Roach, unless, of course, you do have a third?"

Roach smiled, and it was returned knowingly. The one-time naval officer must have had a firm grip on the men under his command, thought Roach.

"You will appreciate that what you have told me requires some degree of consideration. It is well past lunchtime, and I am sure you must both be hungry. I have one or two phone calls to make so that we may proceed in an orderly manner. If you will excuse me, I will arrange for a light repast to be served in this room. We can then get underway this afternoon."

With a courtly bow, the statesman excused himself. Within half-an-hour Sally and Roach were served a pan-fried Gaelic steak accompanied by potato chips, fried onions, mushrooms and peas. The statesman returned hard on the heels of the steward and ate with them, pouring the drinks himself from a decanter of whisky, which he believed "graced the dish more appropriately than wine" and hoping that Sally "would find whisky acceptable", which she did with relish.

He conversed easily throughout the meal on matters of the day: the decline in churchgoing, the nationalisation of the coal industry and the railways after the war, the Queen's coronation in '53, the good harvest of the current year and the likely outcomes of mechanisation in agriculture, the advent of affordable motor cars in the not too distant future, the end of rationing the previous year, the creation of the National Health Service, London smogs, the coming of television. Roach listened politely, aware that his attitudes were being examined and finding that few of the statesman's concerns affected him personally: his family had never been regular churchgoers, he had never seen television or been ill or experienced a London smog and could not foresee the day when he might afford a car, and would usually travel by rail whether or not it was nationalised. But he was greatly impressed with the statesman's breadth of knowledge and his foresight; whatever the distance between them in terms of culture, education and class, he admired the man.

After the meal, Sally and Roach were waved gently to their armchairs, handed a small but elegant brandy and the statesman re-opened their conversation.

"I appreciate your coming and placing your trust in my judgement. Let me say right away that I have no doubt whatsoever regarding the veracity of what you have said."

The sighs of relief from Sally and Roach were almost audible.

"Moreover, I am now going to place my absolute trust in both of you. One of my telephone calls before lunch was to secure a dossier from the office of a friend. This dossier is top secret and access to it is confined to those with a high level of security clearance: that is to say, that any such person will have signed the Official Secrets Act. In fact, few people know of its existence.

I initiated the investigations that form the contents of the dossier because for some years I have been concerned at the increasing number of reports regarding the appearance of an unusual form of aircraft. From the evidence in the dossier, it is quite clear to me that these craft are not of this world. That being the case, they must come from outer space, probably from a planet in our Solar System, and the most likely culprits, until you mentioned the previous existence of the planet you call Minerva, were either Mars or Venus. The dossier contains details of authenticated sightings – all by members of Her Majesty's armed forces: most by RAF personnel but some by the senior service. Men such as these know what they have seen; they do not fabricate stories to draw attention to themselves. All the sightings referred to in the dossier relate to our country.

Let me say, also, that a number of reputable politicians, including one minister, and several senior scientists agree with the findings. It was as a result of these high-placed concerns that the working party to which you referred was established. This was one reason why I was puzzled that I had received no report from them concerning your interview, especially as you have been a serviceman yourself, Mr Roach.

None of us, however, had any notion that the inhabitants of these spacecraft had established bases on Earth. Few events oblige me to deviate from my chosen course, Mr Roach, Miss Tigg, but your findings were an exception. You have both steered us in a new direction for our future investigations; and that is where I want your cooperation. As a corollary to my trust in you I want you to place yours in me. I want you to leave future dealings with these Minervans in my hands and those of my colleagues. I have strong connections with a number of figures in the British military establishment and with senior scientific advisors to the government. We are in a very favourable position to bring this matter to a satisfactory conclusion, but we need to retain the element of surprise and the coordination of our actions needs to be placed in a reliable pair of hands: namely, mine. Do I have your agreement?"

Sally and Roach both gave their assurances with considerable relief, but with Sally pointing out that her livelihood rested in the investigation of unusual phenomena. She would wish to continue her researches and write her articles. The statesman saw no problem with this request provided their recent experiences formed no part of her researches and she refrained from mentioning them in her articles.

"As for you, Mr Roach, I advise you to look to your future. Accept Sir Robert's offer to put in a word for you with De Havilland. They are a well-respected, forward-looking company, and we may expect great things from them in the years to come. They have much to offer a wireless operator and photographer with military experience."

The statesman pressed a bell in one of the panels and within seconds the Chief Petty Officer who had escorted Sally and Roach across London entered with a box file under one arm. Saluting smartly, he left as quickly as he had come.

"I'll leave you for a while. I've a working party to question," explained the statesman with a cold smile.

Neither Roach nor Sally ever revealed by word of mouth or in writing what they read that afternoon in the seclusion of the statesman's club. Searching among Roach's subsequent papers and books, I found not a clue. It wasn't until the full provisions of the Freedom of Information Act came into force in 2005 that I was able to access what is now called *The UFO Archive,* discover for myself the likely fruits of that dossier and supplement Roach's own account of his strange experiences.

Certainly, Winston Churchill's minute of July 1952 to his Secretary of State for Air must have set a few balls rolling: he asked 'What does all this stuff about flying saucers amount to? What does it mean? What is the truth? Let me have a report at your convenience.' Whether it was in response to that enquiry or whether earlier sightings by reputable servicemen provoked the compiling of the dossier, we can only surmise. Churchill had, in fact, ordered an enquiry as early as 1912 when a craft similar in shape to an airship was seen and heard flying over the naval dockyard at Sheerness in Essex.

Three years later, in 1915, a garrison intelligence officer at Devonport, responding to reports from locals that strange lights had been seen over Dartmoor set up a watch. His report describes a bright light ascending to a height of about 60 feet and suddenly vanishing towards the River Dart.

A year later a Flight Sub-Lieutenant took off from the Royal Navy Air Service station at Rochford and was flying at just over 6,000 feet when he saw at a distance of 100 feet what he described as 'a row of what appeared to be lighted windows which looked something like a railway carriage with the blinds drawn down'. When he opened fire with his pistol, the craft disappeared so rapidly that the down swell of air forced his own plane to crash land.

In April 1944 a Flight Lieutenant stationed at RAF Mildenhall in Suffolk, returning from a bombing raid on the steel works of the Ruhr valley, found his Lancaster being pursued by 'balls of light' that with amazing agility were able to duplicate every evasive action attempted by the bomber pilot.

There were many reports of this nature, by both German and Allied pilots, in the archive and one consistent feature of all reports was that the pursuing craft behaved in a 'controlled and intelligent manner'.

A file that must almost certainly have appeared in the dossier was one stamped 'SECRET' with a note indicating that it had been referred directly to the headquarters of RAF Bomber Command. Once again, it involved the crew of a Lancaster who saw a craft, which they estimated to be over 200 feet in length, travelling at 500 mph. The craft had 'four pairs of red lights spaced at regular intervals along its body'. This event occurred in 1942.

Two years later, a radio operator, also in a Lancaster, saw what appeared to be a string of lights on the starboard side of the plane. He described the lights as 'circular, rather like portholes in a ship ... they stretched fore and aft to what seemed infinity ... I could see that they were part of an enormous disc'. All eight crew members saw the craft.

A number of newspaper reports must, undoubtedly, have appeared in the dossier, concerning what were described in true press fashion as 'ghost planes'. One such craft was detected by ground radar at Trimley Heath, near Felixstowe in Suffolk, in 1947. A Mosquito was sent to intercept the craft and pursued its quarry for forty minutes along the coastline of Norfolk. Once again we find in the accounts of the crew a reference to 'efficient, controlled, evasive action'.

As recently as 1954, a pilot flying a Meteor 8 with the RAF's auxiliary air force reported seeing two objects, one gold and the other silver, at a height of 15,000 feet over Chatham. Their speed was such that pursuit was impossible. Looking ahead as they passed his own aircraft, he saw a 'spherical object with a bun above and below' coming straight towards him. At only a few hundred yards distance it suddenly veered to his port side and vanished.

Such incidents appear with alarming regularity in the archive and must have absorbed Sally and Roach during the long afternoon they spent with the statesman's dossier. By the time he returned, they were mentally exhausted

"I trust you have had a worthwhile and informative afternoon, Miss Tigg, Mr Roach. I hope the dossier has supplied some background to the picture you painted for me earlier today. I hope, also, that my making it available to you has cemented the necessary trust between us."

"Yes, of course," replied Sally, "I think you can take that for granted."

A quick smile of gratitude was replaced almost immediately by one of resignation on the statesman's face.

"The specimens you left with our working party seem to have disappeared, Mr Roach, and nobody is able to account for their loss," said the statesman. "Don't look so disheartened, my boy," he continued, noticing utter weariness on Roach's face at these words, "I rather expected this might be the case. Had it not been so, I would have heard about your find long ago."

"Did they have time to examine the pieces of carcase before they disappeared," pleaded Roach.

"Evidently not: they were stored in the laboratory and vanished overnight."

"But they would have taken photographs of the rest of the remains. I told them where the creature was killed."

"By the time a photographer had been arranged and reached the spot – four days after the interview with you – nothing was left of the corpse."

"There must have been traces. A body cannot decompose completely in four days."

"There was no sign of a body or any indication that a body had lain there."

"No shotgun pellets?"

"No shotgun pellets – and that was someone's key mistake, of course. Even supposing the corpse had been consumed by badgers, crows and maggots in that amount of time, the pellets would have remained as would a certain amount of body fluid have been absorbed by the ground. No, no – the corpse was removed as were all signs that one had ever been there. Don't despair, Mr Roach. If anything was needed to convince me that some skulduggery was afoot, the absence of that particular evidence was sufficient. It'll take time because I shall be up against the delaying tactics of the civil service, but I will find out who delayed the photographing of the corpse and who had access to a secure laboratory."

"How did they react to the remains and photographs you took?" asked Sally.

"They were delighted. The working party comprises scientists and intelligence officers from the three armed forces. These are people of integrity. Some scientists are sceptical about this whole business, of course, but they wouldn't suppress evidence ... By the way, your 'gent from Chillesford' has been replaced by another. The house is, once again, occupied."

"When I return for my Bantam," said Sally, "I'll take a look."

"Remember your promise to steer clear of this particular shipping lane, Miss Tigg! Softly, softly, and we shall catch these monkeys. You have my hand on the tiller."

Those last words of the statesman's – whose name I have withheld for diplomatic reasons – were to prove ominous.

CHAPTER 20

The Visitor

Roach and Sally, easier in their minds now that the burden of pursuit had been removed from their shoulders, and having spent the night at Claridges as guests of the statesman, returned to Butley the next day: she to collect her beloved BSA Bantam and return home, he to spend a few more days helping George and Emma restore Creek Cottage before taking up his post as a photographer with De Havilland.

Sally arrived early on the second morning dressed as he had first seen her: a pair of heavy, corduroy trousers and a very large overcoat belted round the waist. George had cycled off to work and Emma and Roach were sitting at the little table in the kitchen enjoying a second cup of tea. Sally removed her hat as she entered; the auburn mane fell to her shoulders and the black, button eyes smiled.

"Not staying. Got a long way to go, but felt I must say goodbye."

"Are you sure you won't have a cup of tea?" asked Emma.

"No, I won't, but thanks. Dot and I were up with the lark. She gave me a good breakfast, and a goodly number of cups of tea – well, you know, I don't want to have to stop too often on the way … Dave, I want to say what a pleasure it's been working with you. I don't think we'll be in touch in the very near future but, who knows, we might one day."

Sally's awkwardness was apparent in the way she spoke and in the hug she gave Dave.

"Have you any immediate plans?" he asked, trying to calm her down.

"I've an idea for an article – not you know what – and an editor friend I knew at Newnham may have a commission for me. We'll see. Anyway, I'll keep busy. Do keep in touch. Drop me a line from time to time. I might be back – who knows. Dot has one or two hauntings to sort out. Suffolk is a great place for hauntings."

And with that parting comment, she hugged Emma, hugged Roach a second time and was gone. Almost before they reached the gate, Emma and Roach heard the BSA Bantam kicked into life and Sally Tigg was a brown blotch on the road. Roach wasn't to see her again for over a year.

He bid his own fond farewells within a couple of days, travelled by train to Liverpool Street and then on to Hertfordshire. The De Havilland Aircraft Corporation was all that the statesman and Sir Robert had promise it would be, and Roach settled down to what should have been the start a new life for a young man. He took digs in St Albans with a family. His landlady had two sons of her own who were about the same age as Roach and he enjoyed their company. Each day he caught the bus to work and the work, which used his skills as a photographer, engrossed him. At De Havilland he met his first real girlfriend, Jean, and they walked out together; his landlady, with a nod of caution, even allowed him to have Jean in his room on occasions.

During that autumn and winter, he wrote once a week to Sally. Although she responded less often, when she did write it was always with some news of the statesman's progress. How Sally acquired the information, Roach never discovered but it always sounded pukka, if vaguely phrased. He learned that Sir Robert had been posted abroad, that the gent from Chillesford's replacement was being kept under discreet surveillance, that Llandrillo had been visited by 'weather station' personnel and that the RAF base commander, Roger Fern, at Bentwaters had been cleared of any connection with the Minervan enterprise.

None of this amounted to much, but it gave Roach the reassurance that something was being accomplished.

Sally also persuaded Roach to undergo a series of hypnotic regressions with a friend of hers. In those days, hypnosis was regarded with deep scepticism; indeed, many regarded it as akin to black magic with one mind (the weaker) being possessed by another (the stronger). In Roach's case, he was able to recall in precise detail the whole of his experiences while held in the Minervan base: experiences that were to supplement his diary entries. The hypnotist (a Harley Street consultant of considerable repute), shaken though he was by what Roach recounted, was constrained by his professional oath from confiding the matter further, and retreated into scepticism.

And then in the late spring of 1956, the newspapers reported a drowning on Bala Lake. At first it appeared that a group of fishermen had met with an accident in unexpectedly stormy conditions, but later it was discovered that a number of naval frogman were involved. The journalists wondered why naval frogman were diving in Bala but Roach and Sally knew, as did Sally's father. A few days later, the newspapers revealed that one of those found drowned was the statesman in whom both Sally and Roach had placed so much reliance.

With that knowledge, Roach's life began to disintegrate. He held onto his job for a time but lost his girlfriend forever. Each weekend became an obsession to seek out the extent of the Minervan invasion. Roach began to collect information on every report that had ever been made of a flying saucer, or any other strange craft, having reached this planet from outer space. Nowadays, such a task may well be undertaken in large part by sitting at a computer and making the right clicks in the right places; in the 1950s and the decades that followed such a search was arduous, involving visits to libraries and newspaper offices, lengthy phone calls (if one possessed a phone), long distances travelled by train and bus, endless letters written and the inevitable 'insolence of office'. The 'law's delay' was, also, to prevent access to much useful information for fifty years!

During that time, Roach's diaries – except for personal entries connected with his research (and more of that later) – descended into annotated records of his investigations. Reading through them after discovering *the* diary of his first contact with the Minervans, I was constantly being referred back and forth to his extensive collection of data, which was kept in box files and folders.

It was soon after the tragedy at Bala that his nose bleeds started. Being of our generation – brought up not to make a fuss about the odd ailment – he ignored them for the most part and got on with his life. This 'just get on with it' attitude turned out to be unfortunate.

It was also after Bala that he and Sally met up again for the first time. An East German acquaintance of hers had read in a local newspaper of 'a disc-shaped craft appearing in the sky'. The craft had seemed about to crash into a hillside north of Leipzig when it had veered skywards 'at an alarming rate'. Moments later there had been 'a tremendous explosion', the craft apparently disintegrated and bits were scattered far and wide. Weekend hikers had made for the hills – one of these being Sally's acquaintance – and returned with pieces of a metal unknown here on Earth: the metal had been 'as light as paper'. Roach and Sally travelled across Europe, eventually arriving at the West-East German border, where a visa obtained for them by the acquaintance secured them access to Communist territory, despite meeting with great opposition from the border guards. A week spent with the acquaintance, during which they enjoyed a long hike in the hills, revealed nothing more, but they did return with the piece of metal. This was subjected to chemical, spectrographic and X-ray analysis. The metal fragment turned out to be a form of magnesium but there were two odd things about it: it did not contain the usual trace elements found in Earthly magnesium but did contain strontium. Nobody was prepared to draw any other conclusion than that the existence of such a metal had never previously been recorded on Earth; the sample was stored for safekeeping. Neither Sally nor Roach saw it again.

Neither did they see much more of each other. Roach had observed a considerable change in Sally: the usually ebullient woman was constrained to the point of being introverted. She was friendly but in a much quieter fashion. She obviously enjoyed the company of both Roach and her East German acquaintance but the conversation had to be drawn from her whereas previously it had flowed. They remained in contact, occasionally collaborating on an investigation, but the burden of responsibility they both felt and their total impotence regarding any action they could take haunted them both.

In 1960, five years after he and Sally's time of trial, Roach's father died, De Havilland became part of the Hawker Siddeley group and Roach seized the chance to give up his job. The reason he gave in his Christmas card of that year was that his mother needed looking after, but this was only a pretext: his real reason was that he wanted to spend more time on his researches. From then on, he took a few part time jobs whenever he needed extra money but lived more or less on social security benefits and his mother's pension. He did become godfather to both my children but as the years gained on us we drifted further and further apart, and had it not been for his occasional long and witty letters might have lost touch altogether. And so his life and mine continued for a quarter of a century.

It was in the summer of 1980 that his diary contains one of those personal (as distinct from annotated) entries that is as startling as those of 1955.

Roach had by now moved to a flat in Borehamwood. His mother, who he looked after and then nursed with a devotion bordering on saintliness, had died five years previously, leaving her and Ernest's house to Roach; with the proceeds of the sale, he decided to move nearer to London and its libraries and museums. The flat was one of a tower block, and was on the sixth floor. He knew few of his neighbours and lived a lonely existence in what he called his 'little library in the sky': every inch of wall space – spare or not – was covered with shelving stuffed with books, box files, folders, reports and the aborted beginnings of the books Roach always intended to write.

He sat reading one night – as must have been his custom on most nights – when there was, first, a ring on his bell and, then, a knock on his door. Roach was startled: he neither encouraged nor welcomed visitors. Besides, the area was known for a degree of mindless hooliganism and opportunist burglaries. He smiled at his own foolishness. What kind of burglar comes knocking? Roach peered through the spyhole that was a standard fitting and saw the distorted figure of just one young man. It had been known, however, for another to crouch below the level of the spyhole. Roach opened the door as far as the chain would allow and was relieved to find no boot thrust into the gap. Peering round the edge of the door he saw a young man, no longer distorted by the spyhole, smiling in what he took to be a hopeful manner and with a shock of thick, auburn hair.

"Mr Roach? Dave?"

"Yes, I'm Dave Roach. What can I do for you?"

The young man reached into the inside pocket of his soft leather coat, removed a wallet and from this selected a photograph. Roach found it difficult to describe his feelings at that moment. He knew the face he would see in the photograph and he knew its relationship to the young man, but he could neither understand nor believe what was happening.

"Come in," he said, without looking at the photograph, "Can I get you a drink?"

"I don't drink," the young man replied.

"Then you'll have to excuse me if I drink alone," replied Roach, "Please sit down. I can't do that alone."

The long silence that followed seemed to be appreciated by both men. Roach sank one, and then another, whisky, while looking at the young man intently.

"You know who I am, Mr Roach?"

"Unlike you, your mother enjoyed a drink, but that hair is unmistakeable. However, I don't understand how you can be sitting in my lounge at all. How is Sally?"

"She died a few days ago. That's why I'm here."

"Excuse me," said Roach, standing suddenly, spilling his whisky and making for the bathroom door.

When he returned, the young man had wiped up the mess and refilled Roach's glass.

"I'm sorry," said Roach, "It was a shock. What happened to your mother?"

"It was a form of cancer. It was very quick."

"I'm so sorry. I cannot say how sorry to hear that news ... I knew Sally well for a brief time and over the years we collaborated on various investigations ... but we ... we hadn't seen much of each other in recent years. Please accept my condolences. I take it that she married? I never knew. She never said."

"No, Mum wasn't married," replied the young man with a smile, speaking as though addressing someone from another age: someone who assumed children were only conceived in wedlock.

"I see," Roach replied, lamely, not wishing to appear condemnatory.

Another long silence followed: the young man seemed not to want to rush Roach into an understanding and Roach was genuinely bewildered. Over the years, he and Sally had collaborated and she never mentioned a son. He looked at the young man closely. He had an amiable face – one that smiled readily – and he had Sally's bright, black, button eyes. The rest of the face was familiar to Roach but it wasn't Sally's – not the nose, not the lips, not the cheekbones: he seemed to know it from somewhere, but could not remember the place. Did he know the father? Roach looked more closely at the young man who smiled back, and when he smiled his eyes sparkled and it was like watching a rainbow dancing.

"Don't be afraid," said the young man.

"Who are you?"

"You know who I am."

"What have they done to me, Dave, what have they done? I'm an old spinster. I'm not going to have children at forty, am

I? What can they have wanted to achieve interfering with me? I have been assaulted by these creatures and I hate them. I've never hated anything in my life until this moment, and the feeling is not a pleasant one." Sally's terrified plea when she had been returned came back to Roach in its entirety.

"Mum never hated me," said the young man.

"You know who ... what you are?"

"Of course. Mum thought that not only correct but also necessary."

"Yes, she was quite right – more than right. Let me think ... Why didn't she tell me?"

"This was 1956. There were no single parents in those days – only unmarried mothers whose children were usually adopted after the mother's confinement in a home for unmarried mothers. You know more about those times than I do, but would I be right in supposing that unmarried mothers were only one step up from a prostitute?"

"Yes," replied Roach, "More or less. It wasn't spoken about in the family, unless the woman was referred to as 'a case'."

"Mum didn't want that, and so I was brought up as her sister's child and I was part of a large family. Mum lived nearby and I saw her every day. She was my godmother and we spent all our spare time together, but people were led to believe that I was my aunt's child."

"It was quite common, I believe," suggested Roach, "Some such children were brought up by the mother's parents as their child."

"It saved the smear of being called a bastard."

"Yes ... She should have told me. We shared so much at that time."

The young man sat quietly watching Roach with those rainbow eyes. There was so much to talk about that Roach did not know where to begin. He needed another drink but his head was swimming from the two whiskies and Roach so much wanted to remain coherent.

"May I get you a coffee … a cup of tea?" he asked.

"Water would be welcome. I've never been partial to hot drinks any more than I am to alcohol."

Roach made himself a cup of red hot tea laced with several spoonfuls of sugar and brought the young man a glass of water. He sniffed it.

"Have you spring water?" he asked, "I do find the chlorine … harmful."

Roach found a bottle in the fridge and poured the contents into a glass from which Sally's son sipped.

"Before she died, Mum made me promise to come and break the news of her passing to you. Would you like to see the photograph?"

"Oh yes … please," replied Roach, "I'd quite forgotten."

The young man as a child of about ten years was in the photograph sitting on a seaside wall with Sally. She looked happy, Roach wrote, and must have been about fifty. There was something familiar about the young man, which Roach couldn't put his finger on.

"When did she tell you about your … heritage?" he asked.

"On the day that picture was taken. Mum considered me old enough to understand and young enough to accept what had happened to her."

"And how do you feel about your heritage?"

"I've never had a problem with being part-Minervan. Can you imagine how quickly I learn? I never had to be told anything twice. It's not just intelligence as your species understands it: it's the collective nature of knowledge and the ability to anticipate. Sometimes at university, I could frame the tutor's question before they'd constructed it themselves."

Sally's son laughed, and it was an amiable laugh. Roach guessed that people would take to him and find him a good listener. Already, a stranger in a strange house, he was beginning to lead the conversation.

"Have you …?"

"No ... sorry, Mum told me not to interrupt just because I knew what was going to be asked; but no, I have not contacted the second species as yet."

"You look quite different in the photograph," said Roach.

"My looks changed dramatically at puberty," replied Sally's son.

"As did mine," said Roach with a laugh, "Can you believe that this dark-haired old man was blond with the face of a cherub until he reached thirteen?"

"As is the boy in the photograph," said Sally's son.

Roach stared hard at the young man, still not comprehending – not quite comprehending.

"Mum didn't see the resemblance until I reached puberty," Sally's son continued, "She'd only known you as a man – not a boy."

"But your Mum and I never ... "

"I know. She was a virgin. I am one of those very unusual occurrences: a virgin birth."

"What's your name?" asked Roach, suddenly realizing he hadn't asked.

"Louis. It was my grandfather's suggestion."

Louis stood up and went to the window. He opened the sliding door and stepped out onto Roach's small balcony, six stories up above the town. It was a clear night, warm and dark and the stars sparkled in the sky as the rainbow danced in the young man's eyes. He stood there for a long while, allowing Roach the time he needed to digest what he had been told.

Sitting in his flat wondering, Roach let his eyes rove across the shelves of books and box files and folders and reports. He remembered: *something was being attached to my genitals and I was aware that I was about to ejaculate.* Had the Minervan's impregnated Sally with his sperm, having adapted the thread of life within one of her egg cells, out of a mischievous sense of humour; or was it more carefully considered as an act of collaboration with the human species?

"Whichever way you look at the issue, there was no consent," said Louis, watching Roach from the balcony door, "And that was neither Mum's fault nor yours."

"No," replied Roach, "I just wish I'd known I had a son."

"I was thirteen by the time Mum realized the possibility – and it was only a possibility, you understand – and I had been reared as my aunt's child. You can see her dilemma."

"Yes, but she should have told me. I deserved to know."

"She wanted you to know... that's why I am here."

"Yes, I can see … Oh Sally, we cannot talk about it now – not now, not ever."

"There's no advantage to be gained from regrets," said Louis.

Roach looked at him, noting the hardness of the remark: a hardness amounting to a lack of feeling.

"I am part-Minervan," explained Louis, "the third species."

"You do regret your mother's death?"

"Yes, you need have no concerns in that regard."

Another silence spread between them, neither being sure what was to happen next. After a while, Louis said:

"What shall I call you?" and smiled as he spoke.

Roach returned the smile, pleased at the young man's human sense of humour.

"I was reared by your species," explained Louis, "and so must share many of your acquired characteristics, whatever others have been unnaturally selected for me at birth. I have much to learn from you before I begin my quest."

"I am certainly more teacher than father", replied Roach, "If you are setting out on a quest, perhaps my role is that of the wise old man."

"Warning me of the perils and temptations that lie in wait?"

"I hope so, but I fear …"

"There is no need to fear," suggested Louis, "Forewarned is forearmed and, unlike Mum and you, I know my enemy."

Roach wasn't sure who that might be, although Louis' face sought to reassure him.

"But first, before we talk, there is Mum's funeral to be undergone and I would welcome your presence."

"You may be sure of that," said Roach, "and if I might deliver the eulogy I should be grateful."

EPILOGUE

The Little Library in the Sky

None of this was known to me, of course, on the day of Roach's funeral. I had never heard of Sally Tigg, let alone her son by Roach. It was only after I had read his diary that I realised Roach was never to know the outcome of his son's quest.

By 1980, telephones were commonplace in the home and my wife answered it one unforgettable morning.

"It's for you," she said, "It's Roach."

The voice on the other end of the line was that of a foreigner. I couldn't place the accent on the phone, but at the funeral found it belonged to Kaamil, a British-born Indian, who told me that he and Roach had been friends for several years following a time when they worked together at the Ministry of Pensions and Social Security.

He gave an oration on behalf of Roach that was both dignified and destiny-orientated. I've never favoured the idea that our destiny is written in the stars. I like to think that we are masters of our fate: that we, and only we, can make the difference on this planet, Earth.

I had already been contacted by Cadge and Gilbert of Radlett, Roach's solicitors, and so Kaamil took me back to Roach's flat after the funeral.

"I found him sitting in his favourite chair," said Kaamil, "He had a book in his hand, a cup of coffee was steaming on the little table and a cigarette smoking in the ashtray."

"He always smoked a pipe when I knew him," I said for no apparent reason.

Kaamil said nothing, but gave me a sympathetic smile as though my opinions were so out of touch as to be almost offensive to my friend.

"What cause of death was recorded?" I asked.

"An embolism," replied Kaamil, and then added as though he wished to spare me such a detail, "He appeared to have had a severe nose bleed."

Kaamil stayed for a while out of politeness and then made his apologies and left me alone in Roach's flat. My wife had been unable to attend the funeral (her health had never been good), and at that moment I was glad: I wanted to be sit, alone and unhurried, where my one-time friend had once called home.

It was then that I found his 1955 diary – the one that recorded the first Rendlesham incident – and sat far into the night reading. It was only later, when I was scouring, painstakingly, through his other papers that I discovered the later diaries and decided to hand all Roach's files over to his son.

I contacted Louis through the number he left Roach and invited him to join me on one of my subsequent visits to his father's flat, which were necessary to complete my executor's duties with his estate.

I liked him at once in the same way I had taken immediately to Roach all those years before, but I had some reservations. While Louis was immediately likeable, he had a single-mindedness that bordered on the ruthless. Having read the diaries, I could not imagine that he inherited that trait from either his father or his mother. I was also aware that he viewed me from a distance, so to speak, as a naturalist might observe the habits of an animal.

My original intention to hand all Roach's effects over to him underwent a revision at that moment. I sat one night while he, too, read Roach's account of the events at Butley and Llandrillo, but kept the diary myself. Louis smiled when I insisted on doing so.

"I understand," he said, "My father was your friend and his diary a memento. You need not apologise. I have memorised every word."

It was during one of my visits to the flat that I called to collect Roach's ashes. The undertaker, somewhat apologetically, took me aside when I arrived and explained that the crematorium had found a strange item amongst "your friend's remains". He handed me a small, silver object that was circular in shape. We both turned it over a few times and shook our heads. Now, all these years on, I can say it was like the batteries one has for hearing aids or watches; then, it reminded us of nothing we had ever seen in our lives.

When I showed it to Louis as I was helping him carry more of Roach's files to his van, he showed the same bewilderment.

"This was found inside my father?"

"Yes, presumably."

He looked at me for a moment and then crossed to Roach's coffee table on which lay that first diary. He flicked through the pages hurriedly, found what he wanted and handed the book to me. I read the extract to which he pointed: *The tube was of some metal substance and at the end of it was a bright light, although whether this was an actual light or merely the reflection from the shiny metal tip of the probe I was unsure.*

"They must have inserted this thing inside his nasal passages so that they could ... who knows ... but we do know he was tracked across the Welsh hills ... What else?"

It was all too much for me. I lacked the young man's need to discover the truth of his birth. I was pleased that he had raised no objection to my keeping the diary and decided to retain that last one also. Young men are impetuous, and I wanted none of Roach's very personal writings to end up in print and be subjected to the common sneer. Written here were the ravings of a madman, fit only for the Sunday papers; at least, that is how the world would see them.

After a few more visits to settle my old friend's affairs, I bid Louis farewell and never heard from him again. Perhaps he wanted to leave an old man in peace; perhaps I was no longer of any use.

The diaries I kept to myself, locking them away in the top drawer of my desk.

Lightning Source UK Ltd.
Milton Keynes UK
UKHW011452131120
373345UK00001B/256